Murder Ridge

K-9 Mystery Series

Bev Pettersen

Published by Westerhall, 2025.

Copyright 2025 Bev Pettersen

Westerhall Books

Editor: Pat Thomas

Paperback ISBN: 978-1-987835-37-3

For my dad, R.K. MacKinnon, who believed in me from the very beginning and whose love and support made everything possible. You are deeply missed.

CHAPTER ONE

A frantic whine cut through the pre-dawn quiet of Los Angeles, echoing off the concrete walls of the storm drain. Nikki Drake crouched at the edge of the opening, her headlamp beam catching the glint of frightened brown eyes fifteen feet below. The dog pressed against the slick wall, trembling but alert, its coat matted with mud.

"Easy," Nikki said softly. "We're going to get you out of there."

Gunner sat beside her, ears pricked. Her K9 partner understood rescue operations, though this one fell outside their usual missing persons work. The call had come from a friend at Animal Control after a concerned citizen reported that a dog was trapped in the downtown drainage system. Most people would have waited for daylight, but Nikki had learned long ago that animals in distress couldn't wait for government hours.

She tested the strength of her climbing rope, checking the anchor point around the steel grating. The storm drain dropped fifteen feet to a concrete channel that would become a raging torrent when the winter rains came. Right now it held only a trickle of murky water and one terrified dog who'd somehow found its way into the maze of tunnels.

Nikki swung her legs over the edge then hesitated. What if this was a sewage drain? The smell drifting up wasn't encouraging. But the whimpering continued, desperate and frightened, and she couldn't walk away from an animal in distress. "I'm coming," she said.

The metal grating bit into her palms as she lowered herself into the channel. Her boots hit the concrete floor with a splash, cold water seeping through the leather.

The trapped dog backed away, hackles raised. Not aggressive, just scared. Nikki had seen that look countless times in animals and people who'd learned that humans couldn't always be trusted. She kept her movements slow, allowing the dog to process her presence.

"Someone's missing you, aren't they?" She pulled a treat from her pocket, the same brand she kept for Gunner. "Bet they're worried sick."

The dog's nose twitched, and Nikki could see now that she was a female, probably a young adult with her lean build. She crept forward to sniff Nikki's outstretched hand, hunger winning over fear. Her collar was leather, well-maintained despite its dirty condition, and fortunately had a tag attached. Definitely someone's pet. Not a stray.

Nikki's phone buzzed against her hip, the sound startling in the enclosed space. She ignored it, focusing on the delicate process of gaining the dog's trust. The animal allowed her to clip a spare leash to the collar, though her muscles remained tense.

Gunner gave a warning bark from above, followed by the sound of approaching steps. "Nikki?" a man's voice called.

"Down here," she said, gathering the rescue line. "Send down the harness."

Minutes later she emerged from the storm drain with a small, muddy dog who licked Nikki's cheek then began scanning the area for familiar faces. Her tail wagged when she spotted the Animal Control Officer, seeming to recognize another helpful human.

"Thanks for coming," Nikki's friend, Officer Martinez said, scanning the ownership tag on the collar and quickly pressing the numbers into his phone.

"Mr. Cameron?" he said. "This is Officer Martinez with LA Animal Control. We have your dog, Buffy ... Yes sir, she's safe and unharmed." Martinez listened for a moment, holding the phone slightly away from his ear as excited voices erupted from the other end. "She was trapped in a storm drain downtown," he said, adjusting the phone. "But an associate got her out ... No, no apparent injuries. Just needs a bath."

The dog's tail wagged harder at the sound of familiar voices coming through the phone speaker, her whole body wiggling.

"You're in Arcadia? Okay, so you can pick her up tomorrow morning, or ..." Martinez paused, raising an eyebrow at Nikki who quickly nodded. She couldn't imagine making someone wait for the reunion.

"Actually," Martinez went on, "my associate is heading in your direction. Would that work?"

After confirming the address, Martinez ended the call and scratched behind the dog's ears, earning a grateful lick. "The owner, Seth Cameron lives in Arcadia. Says Buffy escaped from the yard three days ago. Guy's been posting flyers, checking shelters and vet clinics. Thought he'd lost her for good. You could hear his wife crying in the background."

Nikki grinned, feeling the familiar warmth that came with reuniting families. It didn't matter if the families had two legs or four. The joy was always the same. "I'm happy to drive her home. Heading that direction anyway. Just lend me a crate."

The early morning drive to Arcadia gave her time to decompress. Traffic was mercifully light at this hour, just a few delivery trucks and shift workers heading home. The freeway stretched ahead, downtown's skyline receding in her rearview mirror. She kept the radio low, classical music providing a soothing backdrop as they climbed through the foothills toward the San Gabriel Valley.

Buffy curled in the screened crate, content after enjoying clean water and kibble. Gunner seemed happy to share the back of the hatchback, though he kept a watchful eye on their passenger.

The house was an elegant two story with meticulous landscaping and sweeping views of the twinkling lights spread across the valley. Even in the darkness, it was apparent this was the kind of property that probably cost more than most people could afford.

She had barely parked when the front door flew open and a man in hastily thrown-on clothes came running down the driveway, his bare feet slapping against the pavement. Behind him, a woman in a nightdress hovered in the doorway, one hand pressed to her heart, the door light reflecting the tear tracks on her cheeks.

"Buffy!" Seth Cameron's voice cracked with emotion as Nikki opened the crate and the dog launched herself into the man's open arms. "I thought we'd lost you, sweetie. We thought you were gone."

Nikki watched the reunion from a respectful distance. Moments like this reminded her why her work mattered. Whether she was finding missing children or rescuing trapped animals, the heart of it was always the same: bringing the lost home safely.

"I can't thank you enough." Seth kept Buffy cradled in his arms, the dog's body still vibrating with happiness. "When Animal Control called, I couldn't believe it. Three days we've been searching. I want to pay you."

"No charge," Nikki said. "But please consider making a donation to the local animal shelter. They're always in need of funds."

Seth gave an eager nod. "Absolutely. I'll call them first thing this morning." His eyes sharpened with recognition. "You're that private investigator, aren't you? The one with the search and rescue dog? I read about you and that missing kid case."

Nikki nodded, uncomfortable as always with media attention. "My German Shepherd deserves the credit for that one," she said, giving Buffy a final pat before climbing back into her car.

As she drove home through the quiet streets, Nikki reflected on the night's work. Whether it was a missing child or a dog trapped in a storm drain, the essence was always the same: families torn apart by fear, then made whole again.

She glanced in the rearview mirror at Gunner, who was settling in for a well-deserved nap. He enjoyed the work as well, that drive to protect the vulnerable. It was more than a job for both of them. And these were the cases that reminded her why she'd chosen uncertainty and danger over a steady paycheck.

Her phone remained quiet during the drive home, but she knew the workday would begin soon enough. And as she opened the front door, her phone's buzz announced the start of business hours. She glanced at the screen, immediately recognizing the number. Mountain West Insurance was one of her regular clients, though Patricia Wells rarely called this early.

"Morning, Patricia," she answered, settling into her kitchen chair while Gunner headed upstairs to find Justin, her detective boyfriend who was likely getting ready for his own day of chasing down leads.

"Nikki, thank God you're up early. I've got another one of those cases that's right in your wheelhouse," Patricia said, her voice carrying the familiar tension of someone dealing with a problematic claim. "Remember that horse accident you worked for us up in Mendocino last year? Well, we've got something similar, but bigger. Much bigger."

"What's the situation?"

"Death during a guided horse trip in the Marble Mountains. Woman named Elena Vasquez, riding accident this past spring. Guide's name is Bear Hutchins. Spotless record until now, which is making our underwriters nervous." Patricia's voice took on the clipped efficiency Nikki knew well. "The claim's sitting at three million, and the victim's husband is pushing back on our accident ruling."

"What's his concern?"

"He's convinced his wife was too experienced to simply fall off a horse, or stumble off a ledge. Keeps calling our adjusters, demanding we investigate further. And here's the kicker. Hutchins is taking regular hunting clients out again next week. Same area."

Nikki could hear papers shuffling in the background, Patricia likely reviewing the file. "You know how this works, Nikki. If we can document guide negligence, we deny the claim and drop his coverage. But if this really was just a freak accident..." She paused. "Well, we can't afford to alienate a profitable client over one bad incident."

"So you want me to go undercover. As what? Another client?"

"Safety consultant. We'll tell Hutchins that corporate requires an independent assessment before we renew his policy. It's legitimate. We do that sometimes after major claims. You'll ride along, evaluate his operation. See if he's cutting corners or putting clients at risk."

Patricia's tone sharpened with the calculating edge that made her successful in the insurance business. "Bottom line, we need to know whether we're dealing with negligence or bad luck. The husband's questions aren't going away, and three million dollars is too much to pay out if there's any chance this was preventable."

Nikki swallowed. A week in the wilderness with a potentially negligent guide and his hunting clients. Not exactly a relaxing assignment.

But her mind raced with images of the woman's final moments. The terror of losing control, of feeling a horse stumble, the helpless fall through space. And afterwards, a husband left to grieve, not knowing if negligence or poor judgment had played a role, the victim reduced to a claim number.

She knew what it was like to need answers and not get them. Patricia might be focused on the bottom line, but Elena Vasquez deserved the truth. Nikki leaned back in her chair.

"When do I start?" she asked.

CHAPTER TWO

The morning sun was climbing higher as Nikki pulled into the alley behind her office building, running later than usual after an extended breakfast with Justin. She'd needed the extra time to explain the Marble Mountain case and that she'd be spending a week in some of California's most rugged wilderness.

"That's unforgiving country," Justin had said, his detective's mind immediately cataloging the risks. "The kind of place where accidents happen fast, and help is hours away. Sometimes days if the weather turns."

He'd paused, coffee cup halfway to his lips. "And if something goes wrong, you'll be completely on your own." His tone was careful, knowing better than to suggest she couldn't handle herself. Three years of watching her solve cases had taught him to respect her independence, even when his protective instincts wanted to take over.

His concern had been evident in the set of his broad shoulders, the way his dark eyes searched her face. He understood the unique dangers of wilderness investigations. No backup, no quick extraction if trouble developed, and cell service that disappeared the minute it was needed most.

Nikki shoved aside his concerns and unlocked her office. When she booted up her computer, the email from Mountain West Insurance was waiting. Patricia had been efficient, forwarding everything they had on Dr. Elena Vasquez's death along with detailed files on Bear Hutchins, the guide whose reputation now hung in the balance.

She spread the case materials across her desk while Gunner settled on his dog bed. The bio and photographs of Dr. Vasquez showed a confident-looking woman in her thirties, someone comfortable in outdoor settings. An accomplished researcher and rider with no history of taking unnecessary risks. So what had gone wrong on that spring morning?

Nikki studied the photos, noting the steep terrain and narrow trail. It looked treacherous even in good weather, the kind of place where a horse could stumble. But experienced guides knew how to assess such risks, knew when conditions were too dangerous. And for some reason, Elena's husband was raising questions.

She reached for the phone and pressed the number the insurance company had provided for Dr. Miguel Vasquez. The call went to voicemail, but he returned it within minutes, his voice tight with emotion.

"Professor Vasquez? This is Nikki Drake. I'm a private investigator hired by Mountain West Insurance to look into your wife's accident."

"It wasn't an accident." The words came out flat, certain. "I've told the police, but nobody wants to hear it."

"I'd like to hear it. Could we meet today?"

There was a pause, then the sound of papers shuffling. "I have a faculty meeting until three, but I could see you after that. Do you know where UC Davis is?"

Several hours later, Nikki was driving her Subaru north through the Central Valley, Gunner settled in the back as the landscape transformed. The urban sprawl of Los Angeles gave way to rows of grapevines stretching toward distant hills and the air carried the earthy scent of freshly turned soil.

The University campus sprawled across several thousand acres, its modern buildings and mature trees a stark contrast to the farmland. She and Gunner were both grateful to stretch their legs after the drive and she found Professor Vasquez's office easily enough in the Biological Sciences building.

Miguel Vasquez was a tall, intense man in his forties with prematurely gray hair and eyes that held the hollow look of someone who'd lost everything that mattered. When Gunner entered his cramped office, Miguel simply nodded, as if seeing a working dog was perfectly normal.

The office was cramped with books and research papers, but Elena's presence dominated the space, her photographs covering every available surface. Elena with students in the field, Elena holding various animals, Elena grinning from mountain peaks with research equipment strapped to her back.

"She was the most careful person I knew," Miguel said without preamble, settling behind his desk. "Twenty years of field research. She never took an unnecessary risk. Never."

"Tell me about her work in the Marble Mountains."

"Biodiversity documentation. The university received a grant to catalog how climate change is altering the ecosystems." He pulled out a thick folder. "Elena was perfect for the assignment. PhD in biology, extensive wilderness experience, and she genuinely loved the work."

Nikki studied a photograph showing Elena crouched beside a bubbling stream, camera in hand, focused on something in the water. "What specifically was she studying up there?"

"Everything. Plant species, animal populations, migration patterns. She used trail cameras to document wildlife." Miguel's voice caught slightly. "She was so excited about the project. Said it felt like being paid to explore paradise."

"The insurance file mentions she was an experienced rider."

"Horses were her second passion after biology. She'd been riding since she was eight, competed in college. Elena could handle horses. Could read terrain." He leaned forward, intensity building. "She knew it was important to have a good trail horse. Had even remarked on her horse, a gelding named Brownie, and that she was grateful the guide had given her such a steady mount."

"I understand her guide was Bear Hutchins."

"Yes, and she liked him. Said his base camp was top notch and he gave her space to do her research. He was focused on scouting deer and elk for the fall hunt."

Miguel's face darkened. "Maybe he was too focused. Elena respected local expertise, always deferred to guides. If he'd said the ridge was too dangerous, she would have avoided it."

Nikki made notes, watching the man's body language. Grief could distort memories, make people see conspiracies where none existed. But Miguel's certainty felt genuine, born from decades of knowing his wife.

"Was there anything unusual about her last communication with you?"

"She called the night before she died. Said she'd made an interesting discovery, something unexpected that wasn't part of her original research plan." Miguel pulled out his phone, scrolling through messages. "She used Bear's satellite phone to call me that evening. Said she was riding out early the next day to check her trail cams."

"Any idea what the discovery was?"

"No details. Elena was careful about preliminary findings, wanted to verify everything before sharing. But she sounded excited, like she'd stumbled onto something significant."

Nikki leaned forward, her pulse quickening. "Did she mention working with anyone else? Other researchers, local contacts?"

"Just the guide. She specifically requested him because of his reputation for safety and his knowledge of the wildlife." Miguel's voice turned bitter. "Fat lot of good that did her."

"What about her research equipment? Trail cameras, field notes?"

"That's another thing that bothers me. The Forest Service said they recovered her camera gear, but only the basic equipment. Her trail cams were never found, and her field notebook supposedly disappeared in the fall." Miguel stood abruptly, pacing to the window. "Convenient, don't you think?"

Nikki made notes but kept her expression neutral. Missing equipment wasn't necessarily evidence of murder. Wilderness accidents were chaotic, and gear could easily be scattered. "Equipment often gets lost in falls," she said gently. "The terrain up there is unforgiving."

"But Elena was meticulous about her gear. She kept her notebook in a waterproof case, tucked in the saddlebags." Miguel's voice carried the frustration of someone who'd made these arguments before, to no avail.

"And here's what really doesn't make sense. Her horse survived the fall. They found him grazing in the meadow, without so much as a scratch." His expression softened. "Elena would have been relieved about that. She always said a good mountain horse was worth more than any equipment." Then the pain returned to his eyes. "But if Brownie came through unscathed, why did Elena's gear vanish? It doesn't add up."

"What can you tell me about the other people in the guide's group?"

Miguel returned to his desk, thumbing through his notes. "There were two other men sharing Bear's base camp services. But Elena didn't say much about them. Everyone kept to themselves. They seemed pleasant enough at meals but they didn't interact during the day."

"Did she say anything specific? Were they hunters? Fishermen?"

"I'm not sure if they were together. The guide let everyone do their own thing as long as they stayed on flat land."

Nikki nodded. Shared base camps were a common practice for guides trying to maximize income during the short wilderness season. Nothing unusual about minimal interaction between clients with different agendas.

"Anyone else in the area?" she asked.

"Environmental activists. There's a group that monitors the region, tries to disrupt hunting activities." Miguel's expression darkened. "Elena mentioned seeing them around, said some were quite extreme in their views. She was worried they might interfere with her research since she was camping with Bear's operation."

"Did she feel threatened by them?"

"Not directly. But it was obvious she wasn't a hunter. Her equipment, her behavior, her focus on documentation rather than tracking game. Still, guilt by association." Miguel shook his head. "Those groups can be unpredictable. Elena always said environmental extremists were as dangerous as any other fanatics. Ironically, it was one of their members who found her body."

Nikki's hand tightened around her pen. Environmental groups had been known to escalate their behavior from harassment to violence. A researcher working with a hunting guide might have been seen as a collaborator.

"Professor, I understand your need for answers, but I have to ask: Is it possible this really was just a tragic accident? Remote wilderness, dangerous trail, poor conditions?"

Miguel lowered his head and blew out a ragged sigh. "I've asked myself that question every day for six months. Elena was careful, but no one is infallible. Maybe she misjudged the trail, maybe Brownie spooked, maybe it really was just one of those horrible things that happen."

He looked up, pain evident in his eyes. "But my gut tells me something else happened. Call it intuition, call it denial, but I can't let it go. Elena was planning to call me that evening with details about her discovery. She never got the chance."

Nikki gathered her notes, feeling the weight of the man's grief. Sometimes families needed someone to blame when tragedy struck. But sometimes their instincts were right, and the truth was darker than anyone wanted to admit.

"I'll be up there for an entire week. I'll do my best to find some answers."

"Thank you." Miguel walked her to the door. "And be careful. If what happened to Elena wasn't an accident, then that place is more dangerous than anyone realizes."

The long drive gave Nikki plenty of time to process the conversation. Miguel's grief was genuine, but grief could affect judgment. The missing notebook was suspicious, but wilderness accidents were notoriously chaotic. Environmental extremists provided another potential threat, but they typically targeted hunters, not researchers. Still, an experienced researcher, excited about an unexpected discovery, dead within hours of her last communication. And now the guide was taking clients back to the same area. No wonder the insurance company had concerns.

She'd need to talk to the Wilderness Defense Coalition, the group whose member had found Elena's body, to understand what they'd observed at the scene. She also left a message for Justin asking for information on the Coalition, knowing he could provide information faster than she could dig it up. Years of working cases had given him contacts throughout law enforcement, and his badge opened doors that remained closed to private investigators. Best of all, he would love to help, even if this proved to be a simple accident.

She glanced at Gunner in the rearview mirror. "What do you think, boy? Negligence, accident, or something in between?"

Gunner's tail thumped once, but his eyes remained serious. As if he understood they could be heading into something far more dangerous than a guide's competence check.

CHAPTER THREE

The Wilderness Defense Coalition's office occupied a cramped storefront in Yreka, wedged between a used bookstore and a shop selling crystals. Hand-painted signs in the windows proclaimed messages like "Protect Our Wild Spaces" and "Stop the Slaughter," while faded bumper stickers covered every available surface of the glass door.

Nikki had driven straight up from Davis, following Highway 5 through the agricultural heart of California before turning west into the mountains. The insurance files contained minimal information about the environmental group, just that they regularly monitored hunting activities in the Marble Mountain Wilderness and had been the ones to discover Elena's body. A phone call from Justin had filled in some helpful details.

"Derek Stone, forty-five, multiple arrests for trespassing and harassment," Justin had told her, his voice crackling through spotty cell coverage. "Served six months for chaining himself to logging equipment. Founded the Wilderness Defense Coalition after being kicked out of two other environmental groups for being too radical. Guy's got a serious grudge against hunters."

"Violent?"

"Nothing on record, but he's escalated over the years. Started with protests, moved to sabotage, now talks about 'direct action to protect innocent animals.' Used to be a high school biology teacher until he got fired for bringing students to logging protests. That's when he went full-time activist. Local sheriff considers him a person of interest whenever hunting equipment gets vandalized."

Nikki thanked Justin and ended the call, tucking her phone away as she studied the storefront. The hand-painted signs and bumper stickers suggested passionate activism, and Justin's warning about escalating tactics made her wary.

She glanced back at Gunner in the air-conditioned car. Better to leave him safely secured in the cool vehicle than risk bringing him into what could be a hostile environment. He might raise tensions with people who viewed hunting as animal cruelty, especially if they saw him as a symbol of the enforcement and authority they opposed.

She left her car and crossed the small parking lot, rehearsing what she'd say. Then took a deep breath and pushed open the glass door.

The bell above jangled as she entered the cluttered office. Posters of wildlife covered the walls alongside photographs of clear-cut forests and factory farms. A middle-aged woman with graying braids looked up from a desk covered with petition clipboards.

"Are you here about the elk hunt protest?" the woman asked, her voice hopeful. "We're trying to get the permits revoked."

"Actually, I'm looking for Derek Stone. I'm investigating Dr. Elena Vasquez's death." Nikki handed over her business card. "I'm working for the insurance company that's handling the claim. I'd like to ask him some questions. I understand one of your group found her body."

The woman's expression shuttered. "Derek's in the back. He has an appointment soon but I'll see if he has a minute."

She disappeared through a doorway, returning moments later with a lean man who gestured for Nikki to follow him into the adjacent office.

Despite his outdoor clothing, everything about Derek suggested urban sophistication. The expensive hiking boots, the perfectly fitted technical shirt, the steel-rimmed glasses that gave him an intellectual air. His salt-and-pepper hair was styled in a neat ponytail and he moved with the authority of someone accustomed to addressing audiences. And inspiring people to follow.

"Another investigator? Let me guess. Insurance company wants to blame the victim instead of the hunting guide who got her killed." But he gestured toward a chair, clearly hoping that whatever she discovered might provide ammunition for his cause.

"I'm trying to understand what happened," Nikki said. "Your group found her body?"

"Sage Crux found her." Derek settled into a chair behind the desk, his movements deliberate. "Sage was trying to document hunting violations when she spotted a loose horse at the bottom of a ridge. Found that poor woman's body on the rocks."

"What kind of violations were you documenting?"

"Everything!" Derek's eyes glittered. "Hunters love to break rules when they think nobody's watching. Spotlighting, using illegal baits, hunting outside designated areas. We move around a lot, trying to keep them honest."

"Were you monitoring Bear Hutchins specifically?"

Derek shrugged. "Hutchins has a reputation for catering to wealthy clients who think money exempts them from regulations." He leaned forward, intensity building. "These rich trophy hunters come up from the city, expecting guides to bend rules for bigger kills and bragging rights. And personally, I don't think they should be allowed to use horses. They're not native to the area."

His voice took on the fervor of someone delivering a well-rehearsed sermon. "Real hunters should walk in on their own two feet. Carry out what they kill. Using pack animals is just another way those so-called sportsmen avoid the actual work. They want to play at being mountain men while the animals do the heavy lifting. It's not hunting. It's a luxury glamping trip with guns."

Nikki encouraged him with a polite nod. His passion felt genuine, but there was an underlying current of something harder. "Did Elena Vasquez interfere with your monitoring activities?"

"That woman wasn't a hunter." Derek gave a grudging nod. "We knew she was doing legitimate research. Though I wasn't happy about her using a horse. Sage actually approached her about documenting environmental damage."

"What kind of damage?"

"Habitat disruption, illegal trail cutting, litter and waste left behind. Plus the obvious cruelty to animals. Hunting parties treat the wilderness like their personal playground, destroying ecosystems for entertainment.

"Even llamas, which some people think are environmentally friendly, trample delicate plants that take decades to recover. But they leave permanent scars and disrupt wildlife patterns. The animals can smell them from miles away. It changes their behavior, drives them from traditional feeding areas."

Derek's fervor made Nikki wonder if his group harbored resentment toward anyone using pack animals, including researchers like Elena. "So Sage had contact with Elena before her death?" she asked.

"Minimal. Sage talked to her, explained our mission. Elena was sympathetic but focused on her own research. We respected her work, stayed out of her way. More than I can say for the hunters."

"Tell me about finding her body."

Derek's jaw tightened. "Sage spotted the loose horse, saddled with no rider. Took her a while to hike down. But it was obvious the woman was dead."

"Roughly how long between the accident and discovery?"

"A couple hours. Sage had to hike back to higher ground before she could get cell service to call 911." Derek's eyes shifted, not quite meeting Nikki's gaze. "Rescue teams don't move fast in that terrain. Took them until evening to extract the body."

Nikki noted his evasiveness. There had been plenty of opportunity to remove evidence, like Elena's field notebook or trail cams. "So Sage was alone at the scene for quite a while before help arrived?"

"She stayed with the body the whole time," Derek said then seemed to realize he'd contradicted himself. "I mean, she came back after making the call. Didn't want to leave her alone."

Nikki clenched her hands together, picturing Elena lying broken for hours while help slowly organized. "Did Sage see anything suspicious? Signs of struggle, evidence tampering?"

"What are you implying?"

"I'm asking what your volunteer observed at the scene."

Derek studied her for a long moment, seeming to weigh his response. "Sage said the accident site looked clean. No scattered gear or sign that Elena tried to save herself during the fall. Horse was grazing."

"Was the saddle twisted? Horse cut? Anything like that?"

Derek shrugged, his earlier intensity fading to disinterest. "Sage might remember tack details, but I'm no rider. I just know the damage that horses cause." He waved a hand as if brushing away the questions. "All I know is what she told me. And she's already told the police everything."

Nikki doubted that was true. From what she'd read in the sparse police file, the questioning had been perfunctory. The investigators seemed to have accepted the accident theory, focusing more on Elena's route that morning than on witness details about the horse or tack. No one had pressed Sage about what she'd observed, what condition the horse was in, or whether anything seemed unusual. It was as if they'd been eager to close the case.

"Where can I reach Sage?"

"You can't." Derek's smile was annoyingly smug. "She's returned to the Marble Mountains. It's an important project. Work that requires extended observation."

"Which area of the mountains?"

"Different locations each day. Sage takes her responsibilities seriously. We don't cut corners just because some insurance office suddenly wants useless details."

Nikki nodded but the timing of Sage's assignment struck her as suspicious. Sage, conveniently unavailable just as someone was asking questions about the accident scene. Either Derek was protecting his volunteer or Sage was avoiding investigators for her own reasons. There was no gain in letting Derek know Nikki was heading into that same area. But why would activists want to hurt a research biologist?

"When people contribute to our cause, they expect results," Derek went on. "They're tired of watching hunters destroy the wilderness while authorities look the other way. They understand that we need to take a harder line."

The threat in his words made Nikki stiffen. He was suggesting that his supporters would approve of escalating tactics, including violence.

Derek seemed to sense that Nikki was gathering information that he'd rather not share. "Look, I've told you what I know. Elena didn't deserve what happened to her, but maybe her death will finally open people's eyes to the real dangers of these hunting operations."

The front door chimed before Nikki could reply. A young man in outdoor gear entered, his clothes showing the grime of wilderness camping. But there was something appealing about him. The kind of rugged attractiveness that came from outdoor living rather than weekend adventures. His dark hair was tousled, and when he walked, it was with the confidence of someone comfortable in his own skin.

"Jake!" the woman with graying braids called out, looking up from her desk with obvious pleasure. "Thank goodness you're back. Derek's been waiting for your report."

Jake had the wiry build of a serious hiker. But it was his eyes that would catch any woman's attention. Intelligent and passionate, with the kind of intensity that suggested he cared deeply about things that mattered. When he smiled at the receptionist's greeting, it transformed his entire face.

His gaze took in Derek and Nikki with the quick assessment of someone used to reading people and situations.

"I just need a minute, Derek," he said, his voice carrying both urgency and the respect of someone addressing a mentor. "We need your guidance. Need to know your limits."

Derek held up his hand, silencing the man. "Ms. Drake is leaving. We just finished discussing the biologist's accident."

Jake's gaze sharpened, studying Nikki with new interest before giving Derek a slight nod. The unspoken communication between them was loaded with meaning.

Nikki rose, recognizing the dismissal and knowing that whatever these two needed to discuss, she had no chance of overhearing. She headed for the door.

"Thanks for your time," she said, though Derek had already turned his attention to Jake.

The temperature contrast hit as soon as she pushed open the glass door. The air-conditioned office gave way to late afternoon heat, and she blinked in the sunlight. She was unlocking her car when her phone buzzed with a text from Justin: "Just learned Derek Stone arrested twice for harassing hunters. Released both times due to lack of evidence. Watch yourself around him."

She looked over her shoulder and caught Derek and his rugged visitor watching her through the window. Their stares seemed to be looking for vulnerability. And they made her blood run cold.

She quickly started her engine. In two days she'd drive into the Marble Mountains and join Bear Hutchins and his hunting clients. The same wilderness where Elena had died and where Sage Crux was allegedly conducting her important project. The challenging terrain would cut them off from backup, leaving everyone vulnerable to whatever dangers lurked in those peaks.

Hopefully she'd be able to locate Sage and get straight answers about Elena's accident. Or perhaps, given Derek's disdain for hunters and horses—an attitude his followers likely shared—Sage would find Nikki first. And that might not be a pleasant encounter.

CHAPTER FOUR

———◈———

Evening light filtered through their bedroom windows as Nikki packed her duffle bag, each item chosen for wilderness survival. Bear Hutchins had sent detailed instructions through the insurance company. Everything she brought had to fit in the saddlebags he'd provide, with strict weight limits that forced her to carefully select her gear. The pack horses and their panniers were reserved for the hunting party's food and camp supplies, leaving personal items to whatever could be carried on her horse.

Despite the restrictions, she felt a flutter of excitement as she rolled up her sleeping bag. Although she'd enjoyed plenty of trail rides, she'd never camped for a week in true backcountry, where horses were still the most reliable way to access the land. The thought of spending days in the saddle, navigating mountain trails, appealed to the part of her that felt most alive in challenging places.

Justin sat on the edge of their bed, watching her work. "Merino wool base layers," she said, more to herself than to him, placing lightweight thermal underwear in the bag. "Synthetic insulation, rain gear, orange vest, extra socks." She held up a pair of hiking boots that were also suitable for riding. "And these are already broken in."

Justin's sharp gaze flickered over her belongings. "What about communications?"

"Bear has a satellite phone for emergencies." She tucked her cell phone into a waterproof case, accepting it would only be good to take pictures or to use as a flashlight. "Apparently cell service is non-existent, and even Bear's sat phone might not work in deep canyons."

Justin's jaw tightened. As a city detective, backup was usually minutes away. Patrol units, SWAT teams, helicopter support, all available with a radio call. The idea of her being unreachable for days violated every principle of officer safety.

But Nikki thrived on that independence. Her PI work had taught her to rely on her own skills and Gunner's abilities rather than sophisticated equipment or organizational support. She was used to operating alone, trusting her instincts in situations where help wasn't coming.

Gunner padded into the room, sensing preparation for a trip with the intuition he'd always possessed. Whether it was the sound of the bag's zipper, the way she moved with purpose, or some subtle scent change, he always recognized when they were heading out on a case.

His tail wagged with anticipation as he positioned himself by the door. Nikki had already packed his gear: collapsible water and food bowls, high-energy kibble, a first aid kit, booties and his orange safety vest.

"What about a weapon?" Justin asked.

"Glock 19, three magazines, plus bear spray." She weighed the firearm and ammunition on her portable scale then grimaced. Bear's weight restrictions were brutal, but his warning was legitimate. The rule of thumb was that a horse shouldn't carry more than twenty percent of its body weight, and that had to include rider, saddle, and gear.

She pulled out a heavy flannel shirt and set it aside, making room for her gun. The mountains had black bears and mountain lions, but the possibility of two-legged predators worried her more.

Justin's phone buzzed. He glanced at the screen and frowned. "Something else just came in on Derek Stone. He showed up at the Yreka police station an hour ago, claiming an insurance investigator was trying to harass his volunteer."

Nikki's hand froze over her Glock. "I never told him I was going to the mountains. How does he know I'm looking for her?"

"Good question. The desk sergeant said Stone kept asking if you were 'really just doing insurance work' or if you were working with hunting lobby groups trying to discredit his coalition."

Nikki shook her head. "The guy is paranoid."

"There's more. When they wouldn't give him information, he started talking about a recent case where hunters had been trapped in freezing conditions. Three hunters from Oregon, stranded for eighteen hours after their gear was sabotaged. No one could prove it was Stone's people, but the timing was suspicious."

Nikki felt a chill that had nothing to do with the upcoming mountain weather. "Stranded them how?"

"Scattered their horses, cut tent guy-lines, disabled their GPS units. The hunters spent the night exposed to a late season storm. One nearly died of hypothermia. Stone never admitted direct involvement."

Justin continued scrolling over his screen. "The sheriff thinks Stone's coalition has at least forty active members across Northern California, with cells in different wilderness areas. They coordinate through encrypted communications, share intelligence on hunting schedules, and coordinate disruption campaigns."

Nikki sank down on the bed. Forty dedicated extremists was a small army, especially in remote terrain where they held every advantage.

"When Stone was outside the police station," Justin added, "he made several phone calls. He was overheard saying something about insurance spies heading into our territory and making sure they understand the consequences."

"So he knows I'm going to the mountains." Nikki's mind raced through possibilities. "But how? I was careful not to mention it."

"Maybe he has contacts with the outfitters. Small community up there and word travels fast." Justin moved to the window, peering through the curtains as if expecting surveillance. "Or maybe someone at the insurance company has been talking."

"Either way, he'll be ready for me."

"And he won't be alone. That coalition isn't just a handful of local protesters. It's an organized network with resources and territorial knowledge your guide can't match."

Nikki rose and resumed packing, but her movements were slower now. The wilderness had its dangers, but natural hazards were expected. Human threats were more complex, especially when they involved coordinated groups with violent tendencies.

"Maybe I should inform the local law about potential activist interference," she said, though they both knew the limitations of that approach.

"Stone's relationship with local authorities is complicated," Justin said, stepping closer. "Some see him as a nuisance, others respect his environmental work. And in wilderness areas, jurisdiction gets murky between federal, state, and local agencies. Let me know if I can make any calls that will help."

His hand found hers. "I've got a bad feeling about this one, Nik. Environmental extremists, potentially negligent guide, wealthy clients with unknown experience, and now evidence that you're expected."

"But I already accepted the job, and Elena's husband needs answers."

"I know you won't walk away. Just be careful. Gunner's good, but he can't stop a bullet. And if Stone's people know you're coming, they might turn the tables. Make your group the ones being hunted."

Nikki squeezed his hand, comforting herself as much as him. Tomorrow she'd be heading into the mountains where cell phones didn't work and help might be days away.

"I'll check in whenever I get access to the guide's phone," she promised. "It might turn into a wonderful trail ride that both Gunner and I enjoy."

"Hopefully," Justin said, pulling her close. His arms were taut with a worry he rarely showed. He always insisted on helping, but cases like this were different. He had to watch her walk into danger while staying behind, completely out of contact.

"Just remember," he said, his lips brushing against her mouth in a way that always made her heart skip, "if you discover the biologist's death wasn't an accident, you could become a target."

She murmured acknowledgment and wrapped her arms around his neck, pulling him closer until she could feel his warm skin and catch his familiar scent. Yes, there were a lot of variables. The danger, the activists, the unanswered questions. But tonight belonged to them, and she intended to lose herself in his touch.

Whatever dangers were lurking in that wilderness could wait until tomorrow.

CHAPTER FIVE

The thin motel walls couldn't muffle the sounds of hunters preparing for a dawn departure. Nikki lay in the narrow bed listening to diesel engines warming up in the parking lot, boots stomping on wooden walkways, and the thud of gun cases being hefted into truck beds. The Pine Ridge Lodge had seen better decades, but its location fifteen miles from the wilderness boundary made it the preferred motel for hunters.

She checked her phone: 5:30 am. No messages, and only one signal bar. In a few hours, even that tenuous connection to civilization would disappear.

Gunner stretched on the worn carpet, his internal clock as reliable as any alarm. Through the faded curtains, she watched hunters full of the focused energy of people pursuing their passion. A weathered man in his sixties loaded a compound bow into a pickup truck, his movements economical. Nearby, a father helped his teenage son check a rifle scope, both of them vibrating with excitement.

When Nikki and Gunner descended for coffee, the motel lobby buzzed. Hand-lettered signs covered every inch of available wall space: "Mel's Taxidermy. We Mount What You Shoot," "Buck's Meat Processing, Field to Freezer," and "Lucky Draw Outfitters.

Your Trophy Awaits." The coffee station had become an impromptu gathering point where hunters compared ammunition, checked weather reports, and shared stories from previous seasons.

"Drew a deer tag for Zone D-3," a nervous-looking man in spotless camouflage announced to anyone who'd listen. His gear still bore price tags, and Nikki guessed this was his first serious hunt. "Heard there are some trophy bucks up there."

"Hope you scouted your area first," replied a bearded hunter whose worn clothing and laconic speech marked him as a veteran. "Big bucks don't give second chances."

Nikki filled her travel mug, proud of Gunner for remaining calm despite the activity. Time spent at the track had prepared him for crowded, high-energy environments and she appreciated his steady presence.

They walked outside where the parking lot resembled a staging area for a military operation. Diesel trucks pulled trailers loaded with ATVs, while hunters in various camouflage patterns organized gear. An elk permit holder was rechecking his rifle, still marveling at his luck. "Only drew maybe fifty permits statewide this year," he said to Nikki. "That's why I hired the best guide I could find. Can't waste a once-in-a-lifetime opportunity."

Nikki wished him luck, then tossed her pack into the Subaru's hatchback and eased out of the parking lot. The main highway leading out was busier than she'd expected. Trucks and trailers formed a steady procession toward the mountains, their occupants eager to reach prime hunting areas before full daylight.

Two miles from the main trailhead, she encountered what she assumed were Derek Stone's protesters.

Eight people stood along the roadside holding signs that left no doubt about their position: "Stop the Slaughter," "Protect Our Wildlife," and "Real Men Don't Need Guns." The group spanned several generations, from college-aged activists to gray-haired environmentalists, all united in their opposition to hunting. Nothing identified them as specific members of the Wilderness Defense Coalition, but their presence felt professional rather than spontaneous.

A protester with a megaphone called out to each passing vehicle: "Hunting is murder! Leave the animals alone!" But when Nikki drove past in her neutral-colored clothing with no visible weapons, they barely glanced at her. Clearly she didn't fit their target profile.

She wondered if Derek Stone's coalition members were among the protesters, or if they were already positioned in the wilderness, waiting to implement whatever "reception" they'd planned. Her hands tightened around the wheel and she checked her rearview mirror, memorizing faces of the seemingly peaceful group.

Following Bear's instructions, she passed the main trailhead where dozens of trucks and trailers crowded the parking areas and then veered onto a narrow service road. The pavement gave way to gravel, then packed dirt marked with tire ruts. She was grateful for the Subaru's clearance as the road deteriorated with every mile. The route climbed through dense forest that blocked the rising sun, turning the road into a shadowed tunnel.

The isolation was both beautiful and humbling. But the pristine wilderness also stirred excitement she hadn't felt in months. This was an amazing chance to spend a week on horseback in true wilderness. Her curiosity about Bear Hutchins and his three regular clients was definitely piqued.

Spending a week with four strange men could be challenging, depending on their personalities and group dynamics, but that was part of the job. Whatever tensions or quirks existed within the group, she'd have Gunner for reliable company, and the mountains themselves would be spectacular.

After forty minutes of careful driving, she reached a gravel parking area carved from the forest. The sun had crested the eastern ridges, sending light slanting through the pines and leaving dew-covered spider webs. Mountain jays called from the treetops while the crisp air carried the scent of wood smoke from a distant campfire.

An aluminum gooseneck trailer was parked for easy unloading, and seven horses with hunter-orange halters stood tied to its sides. Bear Hutchins worked among the animals with the efficiency of someone who'd done this countless times. She recognized him from the insurance file photos, though the images hadn't captured his commanding presence.

Bear continued adjusting orange panniers on the second packhorse, barely glancing up. Five horses were saddled, awaiting their riders. It was apparent Bear had been working hard to have everything prepared. Medium height and powerfully built, he had the kind of deep tan that came from decades of outdoor work. His broad shoulders and thick arms suggested the strength behind his nickname, and his hair was cropped short beneath a worn cowboy hat. His truck and trailer showed the quality that came with success in the guiding business.

He finally gave her a nod of acknowledgment but continued securing the pannier with one last hitch. Only when he'd finished adjusting the pack did he approach her car.

"Nikki Drake?" His smile was polite but it faded the second he spotted Gunner. His jaw tightened, transforming him from welcoming host to commanding authority. "Why the hell did you bring a dog?"

"He's part of my investigative team," Nikki replied, knowing she needed to establish her authority. This man reminded her of seasoned cops she'd worked with, not the type to respect timidity or deference.

"Dogs aren't allowed on hunts," Bear snapped. "They cause nothing but trouble. Spook game, chase wildlife and need constant supervision. I should have been told about this."

"I'm sure the insurance company mentioned it in their paperwork," she said, keeping her voice firm. "They hired us as a team. He's a trained search and rescue dog with wilderness experience."

Bear shook his head but they both knew he couldn't argue with his insurance company. "Just keep him from chasing the deer," he said, including Gunner in his dark scowl. "And he better not bother my horses."

"Gunner's great with livestock and has good trail manners. You won't even notice him."

"We'll soon find out." Bear stepped back and gestured over his shoulder. "That's the horse you'll be riding."

He led her to a heavily-muscled bay with a deep chest and a splash of white on his forehead. "Twelve-year-old Quarter Horse cross, one of my most experienced," he said, scratching the horse's neck with open affection. "We mainly use him for female riders. Name is Brownie."

"So this is the same horse Elena Vasquez rode?"

"Yup, I thought it would be the best way for you to evaluate the horse. But like I told the insurance company, it couldn't have been Brownie's fault. And I don't see why you have to come out here and second-guess the police report. Elena must have dismounted, then slipped."

"With a big claim," Nikki said, "insurance companies have to be thorough. It's not personal, just due diligence. They need an independent assessment to close the file." But she noted his cooperation. Putting her on Elena's horse showed confidence in the gelding and a willingness to let her see firsthand what the researcher had experienced.

"All my horses are trailwise," Bear said. "Otherwise I don't keep them." He eyed Nikki's height and then proceeded to adjust the stirrup length. His help was appreciated as western stirrups were harder to change than English tack. He stepped back, his face creasing in a grin that made him seem more approachable.

"Brownie will love that you're nice and light," he said. "But go ahead and load up your stuff. See what doesn't fit. And from now on you're responsible for his care and saddling. Keep the halter on beneath his bridle and always pack your hobbles. It's convenient when you want to stop and if he's not saddled, the orange halter will keep him safe."

Nikki nodded, noting the orange pads beneath the saddles as well as the fluorescent orange panniers on the pack horses. Bear clearly took hunter safety seriously, outfitting his entire operation with high-visibility gear. The insurance company would be pleased to hear about these precautions. It showed a guide who understood liability and took reasonable steps to prevent accidents.

She transferred her gear to the leather bags attached to the rear D-rings of Brownie's saddle, conscious of Bear's scrutiny. A pair of hobbles was already in the saddlebags, but other than that they were empty. It was a good thing she'd packed carefully and weighed each item beforehand. Her organized efficiency paid off.

"Well done," Bear said, watching her finish. "It's obvious you know horses. Some clients overpack then complain that their horse is lazy. They're not machines. And you did a good job balancing the weight on both sides. Here, I'll help you tie your sleeping bag."

His helpfulness seemed genuine yet she wondered how much of his sudden warmth was calculated. Her report to the insurance company could make or break his reputation. A guide with documented safety issues could find himself without clients, while one with insurance company approval could command even higher fees.

The sound of a vehicle broke the quiet. A luxury SUV bounced over the deep potholes, approaching way too fast considering the tied horses.

"Sorry we're late," called the driver as three men climbed out. "Damn protesters had the road blocked. Wouldn't move even when the sheriff showed up. One of them actually threw something at my windshield." He gestured toward a spider web crack in the glass. "Deputies had to drag them off the road. Bunch of screaming lunatics, calling us murderers."

The man slammed his door harder than necessary. "They had our license plates. Taking pictures, writing things down. Made it personal."

Bear's jaw tightened, his callused hands stilling on the pack rope. "How many?"

"At least a dozen. Maybe more in the trees with cameras. They're getting crazier every year."

Bear sighed, his gaze shifting toward the mountains. "If they're documenting vehicles, they might have people positioned along my regular trail. So far they've left it alone but they could make things complicated."

He looked at Nikki, his expression troubled. "Coalition's been escalating their tactics. Last month they sabotaged tree stands in Colorado, nearly got a hunter killed." He noticed the men's sudden quiet, their curious stares. "This is Nikki Drake," he said, jabbing his thumb. "Insurance researcher. She'll be coming along, observing our safety protocols."

The timing of her presence suddenly felt awkward. If activists were aggressively targeting hunters, Bear's operation was already under scrutiny. The last thing he needed was an insurance investigator documenting possible safety lapses.

She could only imagine his simmering resentment, forced to accommodate someone who could destroy his livelihood with a single report. And his clients probably felt equally invaded, their retreat shadowed by a woman noting their every move.

She hid her concerns behind an easy smile as Bear made introductions. "Nikki, meet Marcus Webb, Ryan Torres, and Doug Lohnes."

Marcus strode closer, his polished appearance incongruous with the forest setting. Even in outdoor gear, everything about him suggested urban sophistication: styled hair, gleaming teeth, and a hint of expensive aftershave. His confident smile and commanding presence marked him as someone accustomed to being the most important person in any room.

"Then we need to renegotiate the rate," he said to Bear. "Our fall contract was based on an exclusive booking. An additional person wasn't part of our agreement."

Ryan and Doug nodded but hung back, as if used to letting him handle their negotiations.

"I sent you all an email yesterday," Bear said. "This is insurance company requirements after the accident. Price stays the same."

"But what about the dog?" Marcus asked. "You've always maintained a strict no-pets rule."

"Requirement of the insurance company." Bear's flat tone showed the discussion was finished.

Marcus stared at Bear, his jaw tight with displeasure. Then he turned to Nikki with a practiced smile, the kind that managed to be both charming and condescending without being too obvious. "No offense, Nikki," he said.

Bear watched this exchange in silence, his weathered face revealing nothing. Only when Marcus turned away did Bear speak again. "Let's get you matched with your horses," he said. His tone had an underlying edge that suggested Marcus often tested his patience.

Bear pointed to a sturdy chestnut gelding. "Marcus, you're on Thunder. Ryan, take Scout. He's the gray. And Doug, you're riding Scooter, the same horse you rode this spring."

Nikki's pulse quickened with interest. Elena's husband had mentioned two regular clients at Bear's spring camp, hunters who'd focused on scouting game. However, no names had appeared in the insurance files. If Doug had been present, he might have some insight into what had left Elena so excited. Even if they hadn't had the same interests, they'd likely shared meals.

Bear's crisp voice cut through her thoughts. "Ryan, that's too much weight. I warn you every time about bringing so much equipment."

"But I need a good camera." Ryan clutched a bulky black case he was trying to stuff in a saddlebag. "Can I put it in one of your panniers?"

Bear sighed. "The pack horses are already carrying our supplies. Is that thing essential?"

"Absolutely," Ryan said.

While the two men negotiated pack space, Nikki grabbed the chance for Gunner and Brownie to meet. She motioned Gunner closer, keeping one hand on his head and the other on the horse's shoulder. The gelding lowered his head, nostrils snuffling, while Gunner wagged his tail.

"Good boys," she murmured, reassured when Brownie remained relaxed. Making sure they were comfortable now could prevent problems later. The last thing she needed was Gunner getting kicked, miles away from vet care. But both animals were perfect gentlemen, and she was able to turn her attention back to the hunters.

All three of Bear's clients appeared to be in their forties, but the differences became apparent when they approached their horses. Marcus moved with the confidence of someone who often hunted on horseback. His scarred rifle scabbard suggested encounters with rocks and trees, and he swept his horse with a knowing eye.

"Thunder's looking good, Bear," he said, running a hand along the chestnut's rump. "Put some weight on since last year. Good muscle development too." He stepped back, clearly pleased with his assessment.

On the other side of Marcus, the man named Doug loaded his saddlebags in silence, his pale skin suggesting more time spent indoors than his companions. But his rifle looked expensive and he scanned his surroundings like someone used to calculating range and wind. The kind of man who would only need one shot to bring down his target.

She checked on Ryan who seemed the least experienced of the group. He'd convinced Bear to carry his camera equipment and now fumbled with his horse's cinch. Nikki noted that unlike his two friends, he had no scabbard.

"Do you have a deer tag?" she asked, giving him a friendly smile.

Ryan chuckled. "No, I'm the designated photographer. Someone has to document Marcus's tall tales. Beautiful dog," he added.

He was the most genial of the three and had a quick smile. Gunner even tolerated Ryan's pat, which improved Nikki's opinion of the man. The group dynamic seemed simple: old friends comfortable with each other's quirks and successful enough that they could afford a guide's services.

But there were undercurrents. She'd caught the glance Marcus and Doug exchanged when Bear mentioned Elena's accident. A look that lasted a fraction too long, loaded with meaning she couldn't decipher. And though Marcus had smiled after demanding the discount, his eyes had remained cold.

Doug's measured words intrigued her the most. He wasn't just quiet; he was cataloging. The three men moved around with the easy familiarity of long friendship, and it was clear she'd be the outsider in this tight group. At least she had Gunner on her side.

She lowered the zipper on her jacket. The sun had climbed higher, warming the air and drawing the scent of resin. A woodpecker's drumming echoed from the forest, punctuated by the chatter of squirrels. The horses shifted, eager to move after standing tied for so long. But it was another ten minutes before Bear completed his final check, confirming the pack horses' loads were secure and checking each breakaway link.

"Time for the safety briefing," he announced, launching into trail etiquette and emergency procedures with the rhythm of someone who'd given this speech hundreds of times. The other men continued their preparations—tightening cinches, rolling slickers—clearly familiar with every word. Nikki suspected the lecture was either for her benefit or for the insurance report she'd eventually file.

"And no shooting from your horse," Bear said. "They're unpredictable animals, not machines." His gaze swept each rider, deadly serious now. "Saddle slips, your horse goes down a cliff with your foot stuck in the stirrup. Maybe he spooks at a rattler and you're bucked off. Or he steps in a gopher hole. Then you're walking out twenty miles with a lame animal. Or putting him down where he stands."

He tugged his cowboy hat lower. "Pack horses can get spooked by a bear, scatter our gear across two square miles. Then you're sleeping under the stars with no food or water, hoping someone finds you before the weather turns. That's why you listen to everything I say. These mountains don't give second chances."

His eyes found Nikki's, and she caught a flicker of something, regret or concern, before the brim of his hat shaded his expression.

"Weather's supposed to hold for the rest of the day," he said. "We've burned enough daylight. Time to move out."

He strode toward his horse, a handsome buckskin that stood patiently beside the two pack animals. Bear deftly gathered the lead ropes and swung onto his horse, then called over his shoulder. "Nikki, you and your dog can bring up the rear. The only horse that might kick is the gray. Scout's had a few encounters with coyotes, so make sure your dog keeps his distance."

Nikki nodded, relieved to finally mount. She settled into Brownie's saddle, happy to find it didn't force her legs achingly wide. The leather was supple, the seat soft and cushioned, and the stirrups properly adjusted. So far Bear's competence couldn't be questioned. Everything from the horses' condition to his careful supervision spoke of a professional who took care of his clients.

On the other hand, Elena Vasquez had died on his watch. Nikki pulled in a long breath, imagining the horror of the woman's last seconds, her desperate scramble to grab a root, the sickening sensation of empty air. Something unexpected had happened on that ridge. Maybe her fall hadn't been due to Bear's negligence. Maybe she'd encountered an overzealous activist, one who thought scaring her horse was justified.

Nikki resolved to keep an open mind, as well as stay alert. It was a bonus Bear had assigned her to the rear. Gunner would be safe, and she could keep the other riders in sight. More importantly, people often forgot about riders behind them. They'd start talking, assuming they were out of earshot, not realizing how sound carried. Some of her previous breakthroughs had come from conversations people thought couldn't be heard.

And this wouldn't be all work. Time spent on a horse should be relished, especially in country this spectacular. For now she was content to settle into Brownie's ground-covering walk and follow the string of animals.

They filed past a Forest Service sign mounted on a wooden post, its green background bleached pale by altitude and sun, warning about white-nose syndrome in bats. The sign noted that caving remained unmonitored, a reminder that these mountains were still wild and unforgiving. Nikki felt the truth of those words as she noted the towering granite walls ahead. Soon, they would be completely on their own.

CHAPTER SIX

The trail climbed through dense forest, forcing the riders into single file as the path narrowed between towering pines and rocky outcroppings. Nikki settled into Brownie's rhythmic stride, the gelding's steel shoes ringing against the rocks. The metallic sound echoed off the canyon walls, mixing with the creak of leather and the heavy breathing of horses.

The crisp air carried the scent of pine needles crushed underfoot and the earthy smell of decomposing leaves. Gusts stirred the aspen trees, sending leaves spiraling down to catch in Brownie's mane. The temperature was perfect for riding. Cool enough to keep the horses comfortable on the climb, warm enough that Nikki had left her jacket unzipped.

From her position at the rear, she could see the entire group. On the straighter sections, Bear was visible. His stocky buckskin moved with the composure of a good lead horse, undaunted by loose rocks and fallen branches, and the two pack horses dutifully followed.

Gunner trotted alongside Brownie's left flank, sniffing at the variety of scents. A squirrel dashed across the trail, barely two feet away, but he merely watched it dart up a nearby tree. His experience showed in his behavior, alert to everything but not distracted by wildlife.

The wind carried fragments of conversation from the riders ahead. Doug and Ryan were discussing the logistics of reaching base camp, their voices drifting back on the breeze.

"Hope we make it before dark," Ryan was saying as they navigated around a sharp switchback. "I'm already sore."

"Should be fine if we keep this pace." Doug spoke in the same measured tone she'd noticed at the trailhead. "Weather might get chilly though."

"Do you think Bear brought steaks?" Ryan asked, and she could hear the anticipation in his voice. "I'm looking forward to a good camp meal."

Their conversation seemed focused on the trip, lacking the undercurrents she'd sensed earlier. Maybe she'd been reading too much into their behavior. Or maybe they were simply being careful about what they discussed.

She plucked another leaf off Brownie's mane then tested his training, asking him to move sideways. He shifted from her leg pressure with the responsiveness of a dressage horse, minus the drama. Impressive, and a necessary skill for a horse who might have to avoid an obstacle. But often trail horses were herd bound, used to following the horse in front. Maybe Brownie had turned skittish with Elena when he was alone on the ridge.

Nikki waited until the trail curved around some trees, and Ryan and Scout vanished. Then she tightened her reins, holding Brownie back. He stopped, showing no anxiety. His stoic acceptance was notable. Horses were herd animals and many became agitated when left alone. But Brownie remained unfazed as if accustomed to a rider's whims. The amount of training needed to produce this type of reliability was considerable, and it also underscored Brownie's level mind.

She stroked his neck in approval then urged him forward to catch up with Ryan, who remained oblivious to her brief stop. The geologist sat crooked in his saddle, leaning forward with an awkward slant to his arms. Every time Scout broke into a trot, he bounced in the saddle, unable to find the rhythm that would make the ride smoother for both him and his horse.

She followed Ryan and Scout through a stand of ancient pines. Their massive trunks created cathedral-like columns, filtering the sunlight into narrow shafts. Years of fallen needles carpeted the trail, muffling the horses' steps and creating an almost reverent quiet.

In this setting, it was hard to imagine tragedy striking. Yet Elena Vasquez had ridden this same horse on the same mountain. A woman conducting legitimate scientific research, riding a calm, well-trained gelding and directed by an experienced guide. The more Nikki learned, the less Elena's death seemed like a simple accident.

She filed that thought away as the trail demanded her full attention. The path had narrowed considerably, winding between granite outcroppings where loose shale could send a horse scrambling. Fallen logs blocked sections of the trail, forcing them to navigate around obstacles, while roots created natural tripping hazards.

After another hour of climbing, Brownie's neck was slick with sweat, but he maintained his ground-covering walk. She kept light contact with the reins, helping him stay balanced as they navigated the increasingly challenging terrain. When the trail steepened dramatically around a switchback, she shifted her weight forward, making it easier for him to drive upward with his powerful hindquarters. His breathing had deepened with the effort, but his steady rhythm never faltered. Clearly he was well-conditioned.

The sun was almost overhead when Bear raised his hand, signaling a halt. They'd reached a clearing where a stream cut across the trail, and Brownie quickened his stride, as if recognizing a familiar rest spot.

"Let them drink," Bear called, swinging down from his buckskin. "Dismount, give their backs a break. Let them have a bite of grass. We've got another two hours to base camp."

Nikki stepped down, leading Brownie upstream from the other horses. Gunner followed, lapping gratefully at the clear water while Brownie lowered his head for a long drink.

Bear gave her an approving nod. "Smart. Always water upstream when you can."

His pleased expression faded as his gaze moved past her to the soft earth beside the bank. Nikki followed his stare and felt her stomach tighten.

Fresh boot prints marked the mud. Several different sets, their edges still sharp. The treads were deep, suggesting heavy packs, and the stride patterns indicated people moving with purpose rather than casual hikers.

Marcus noticed their attention, his eyes narrowing. "Activists? Well, that might impact our timeline."

Doug led his bay horse closer. "How fresh do you think they are?"

"Recent," Bear said. "Maybe this morning. They could be just ahead." He straightened, scanning the trees with the wariness of someone who expected unwelcome visitors. They'd all seen the activists earlier, and now it looked like their paths would cross again.

Nikki motioned to Gunner, who sniffed at the prints, processing the scents. If whoever made these tracks was still in the area, he'd let her know.

"Can your dog follow a trail?" Doug asked, surprising her with his interest. It was the first time the taciturn man had addressed her, and his question caught her off guard. "If you wanted to track someone?"

She kept her response casual, not wanting to reveal the extent of Gunner's capabilities. "He has a good nose, but we're not here to track hikers."

Doug nodded, though his gaze lingered on Gunner with an unreadable expression. "Good to have him along. Extra security."

Even Bear gave a grudging nod. All three men studied Gunner for a moment while Ryan remained downstream, absorbed in splashing water on his face. His indifference to their discovery struck her as typical. He seemed to defer problem solving to the others, especially Marcus.

Bear's voice pulled back her attention. "Mount up," he said, straightening the pack horses. "We're skipping the usual lunch break." He pulled trail bars from his pack and tossed one to each rider. "Keep moving and stay alert. If you see anything that doesn't belong, sing out."

Brownie had already begun to graze, clearly expecting a rest stop. His surprise at being asked to continue proved that Bear's schedule was based on routine. If the horses knew when to expect breaks, anyone watching the guide's operations would also know. But with the stop cancelled, it might be possible to catch the activists in the middle of whatever sabotage they might be planning.

They continued riding up the steep trail. The horses had to work harder, their breathing more labored. The forest thinned as they gained elevation, offering a better view of the towering peaks. The cliffs caught the afternoon light, creating a backdrop of gray and gold that would have been breathtaking if she wasn't already on edge.

A sharp shout from ahead brought the riders to a sudden halt.

"Dammit!" Bear's angry voice carried down the trail.

Nikki couldn't see the cause of his outburst, but heard him dismount, his boots hitting the ground with unusual force. The pack horses tossed their heads, picking up on his agitation.

"What is it?" she heard Marcus ask.

"Wire," Bear replied. "Stretched across the trail."

Nikki rose in her stirrups, straining to see past the line of horses. Between the shifting bodies, she caught a glimpse of Bear crouched beside the trail, wire cutters glinting in his hand.

"Wait!" she called, moving Brownie closer. "Take a picture before you cut it."

Bear paused. "You're right," he said, pulling out his phone.

He snapped several photos before cutting the wire, a thin gray line that was nearly invisible against the rocks. It had been strung six inches from the ground, positioned to catch a horse's leg just above its fetlock.

"What assholes," Marcus muttered, shaking his head. "That wire could have broken a horse's leg. Maybe hurt one of us in the fall."

"Could hurt their precious wildlife too," Doug said. "Deer use these trails at night. Doesn't seem rational."

"It's not rational," Bear growled as he coiled the severed wire with jerky movements. "They're not just waving signs anymore. They're actively trying to hurt my horses."

He took a deep breath, visibly forcing himself to focus on gathering the pack horses' lead ropes. But when he swung into the saddle, his face was mottled with anger. "I'll notify the Forest Service tomorrow morning. I can usually get a satellite signal in the meadow."

They resumed their climb in silence. The earlier fragments of conversation about camp meals and weather had disappeared, replaced by a tense quiet broken only by the strike of shod hooves on stone. Even the horses seemed subdued, affected by their riders' unease. The only voice now was Bear's occasional warning about navigating a fallen limb or loose rock.

Nikki found herself studying every shadow, every unusual shape along the trail. The tripwire revealed a chilling level of premeditation. Someone had hiked into these mountains carrying materials designed to injure horses. And riders.

The discovery deepened her suspicions about Elena's accident. Had the researcher encountered similar sabotage? But why would activists target someone who clearly wasn't a hunter? Each step deeper into the wilderness only raised more questions.

CHAPTER SEVEN

Brownie's head rose, his steps quickening, and Nikki guessed they were close to their camp. Minutes later, they crested a low ridge where the trail spilled into a lush meadow. To their left, a crystal-clear stream bubbled, its surface catching the light filtering through the aspens.

The trees surrounding the meadow blazed with fall color while the air carried the bite of approaching winter, clean and sharp. This high in the mountains, the temperature would drop fast once the sun disappeared, and it was a relief to see that the campsite was ready for them.

Bear had clearly spent a lot of effort developing the site. A stone-lined fire pit sat in the center of the clearing, complete with wind screens offered by granite slabs and a large log for a sitting area. A tether line stretched between two solid pines, and weathered poles of a small corral were tucked against the trees. Canvas tarps hung ready to deploy from anchor points, creating a temporary lean-to if weather turned rough.

The setup reflected the expertise of someone who understood wilderness camping. Every detail had been considered, from the sheltering cliff to the presence of good water and grass.

"Finally!" Marcus raised an arm in the air. "I was starting to think we'd be riding in the dark."

"Perfect timing," Ryan added, his relief evident as he rubbed at his lower back. "I forgot how much work it is to get here."

"Let your horse drink first," Bear called. "Then we'll get them unsaddled and give them a chance to graze."

Gunner had been sniffing the ground beside Brownie but suddenly his body stiffened, focused on something beyond the corral. His short bark cut the tranquility.

Bear scowled at the sound then checked the trees, his expression shifting from irritation to alertness. Nikki saw something too. A flash of movement between the aspens, gone so quickly it might have been imagined. Except Brownie and Bear's buckskin were also staring in that direction, their ears pricked with the awareness that had kept their species alive for millennia. As flight animals, horses preferred open spaces where they could see danger coming. When they focused intently on dense cover, there was usually a reason.

"Guess the activists didn't expect us to arrive so early," Bear said, already wheeling his horse. "Marcus, hold the pack horses. Come with me, Nikki, and bring your dog. Let's go meet our visitors."

Nikki's pulse quickened as she gathered her reins, eager to let Brownie stretch into a gallop. Bear's willingness to include her in a possible confrontation sent a thrill through her. But the rifle strapped to his saddle was a sobering reminder that this wasn't a casual ride. They had no idea what weapons the hidden visitors might be carrying, or how far they were willing to go to disrupt the hunting operation.

They urged their horses through the trees, Gunner racing ahead with enthusiasm. The horses' hooves pounded against the ground, creating a drumbeat that would announce their approach. Nikki kept a wary eye on the ground, watching for gopher holes beneath the fallen leaves. One wrong step at this speed could send Brownie tumbling.

But within minutes, they were forced to a halt. A granite wall rose ahead, its face too sheer for horses to climb. Gunner cast around the base, then sat, staring upward in disappointment.

"No point continuing on foot," Bear said, straightening in the saddle. "It's a rough climb. And my responsibility is back at camp. Besides, this is public land. People have a right to be here, even if it's unusual."

"Unusual?" Nikki asked, guiding Brownie around as they headed back toward camp. The word carried grim implications, and she found herself scanning the ridge one more time, searching for whoever Gunner had detected.

"I picked this spot because it's hard to access. Most people choose areas closer to good trails. Been bringing clients here for eight years, and we've never had much company."

"Now they seem to know everything about you," Nikki said. "Even your schedule."

"Seems that way." Bear grimaced. "Guess it's a natural result of Elena's accident. It's fired the activists up, provided ammunition."

He shortened his reins, checking his prancing buckskin, who still seemed keen to run. "If I can just get through the season and your report clears me, things should die down over the winter. Activists are quick to move on. They depend on public opinion to grab people's hearts. Save the whales, protect the seals, that kind of thing. Abstract arguments about hunting rights don't generate the same response as a cute animal in danger. Or a tragic accident like Elena's."

A muscle twitched in his jaw, and Nikki realized that Buck's horse wasn't prancing because he was excited. The buckskin sensed his rider's emotions.

"The insurance company already has me classified as high risk," Bear admitted. "They're prepared to dump my coverage." He met her gaze, his eyes dark with concern. "Can't work without insurance. No coverage means no clients. Twenty years of building this operation. Gone."

The weight of his words settled between them. Whether Elena's death was truly an accident or something more sinister, Nikki's report could end Bear's career. His entire livelihood hung in the balance.

And it left her gut in knots. She liked Bear. He was professional, knowledgeable, and clearly cared about his work. One of the reasons she preferred search and rescue to insurance jobs was because she enjoyed helping people. The work was cleaner. Find the missing person, reunite families, save lives. But this investigation felt murky, full of competing interests where good people might get hurt.

They rode back to camp in silence. Marcus waited, still holding the lead ropes of both pack horses, but his impatience was obvious in the way he shifted his weight from foot to foot. As someone clearly accustomed to being in charge, he resented being left behind. His expression suggested he considered himself second in command and expected to be consulted, even if it was Bear's hunting party to lead.

"Well?" Marcus demanded the moment they were within earshot. "Who was it?"

"Couldn't tell," Bear replied. "Too steep to follow. Hopefully just hikers."

"Too bad we couldn't scare them off ourselves. We don't need forest officers up here, poking around. Maybe you should rethink making that tripwire report."

"That's right," Doug said. "Deer hear people moving around, they might disappear for days."

Nikki's hands tightened on her reins. Most people would be worried about safety threats, but Doug and Marcus seemed more focused on how this would impact their hunting.

"Let's get the horses settled," Bear said, clearly choosing to shut down the discussion. "Sun's dropping fast."

Marcus and Doug exchanged looks, their disgruntled expressions making it clear the subject wasn't over. It was apparent they didn't want Forest Service personnel or activists tramping around. To them, there was nothing worse than having strangers spook a trophy buck just as they're lining up a shot, or having government officials questioning every move in what should be isolated hunting territory.

Bear simply scooped up the pack horses' lead lines and turned his attention to the animals, effectively ending the conversation. His body relaxed as he shifted into his element, moving with the efficiency of someone at home with horses.

The next hour was a master class in wilderness horse care. Bear lowered canvas bags from a cache high in the pines, producing brushes, hobbles, and supplemental feed with the efficiency of someone who'd designed the system.

"Horses first, always," he said, demonstrating the importance of brushing away the sweat marks left by the saddle. "They've been carrying us all day. Least we can do is make them comfortable."

He helped Ryan with the hobbles, reminding him how to place the leather straps around the horse's front pasterns. Ryan was clearly uncomfortable crouching beside Scout's legs, his movements tentative as he fumbled with the buckle.

"Like this," Bear said, demonstrating the technique for what was clearly not the first time. Despite having shown Ryan the same method on previous trips, Bear revealed no irritation, his voice remaining instructional. "Make sure they're snug but not too short. You want them to be able to graze but not wander far. And never hobble near cliffs or obstacles. A hobbled horse can't maneuver as well if they get spooked, so you need safe, level ground."

He moved to check Nikki's work, nodding approval at her hobbling of Brownie. "Good. You've done this before."

"A few times," she said, not mentioning that her boyfriend was an expert at anything horse related. And most other things as well. She experienced a pang, already missing Justin's reassuring confidence and the way he made everything seem manageable. He would have enjoyed these mountain trails, the challenge of the terrain, the quality of Bear's horses.

She'd call him in the morning, assuming she could get reception and Bear would allow the use of his satellite phone. Many outfitters discouraged personal calls to maintain the wilderness experience. It would be best to make the call sound work related, perhaps a check-in with her office about the insurance investigation. Bear seemed reasonable enough to understand the need for professional communication.

Not that she needed a homicide detective's advice. She was perfectly capable of handling this investigation. But hearing Justin's deep voice would ground her, remind her that there was a world beyond these mountains where people weren't setting wire traps or lurking in the shadows.

"The horses won't try to travel much when they're hungry," Bear said, pulling back her thoughts. "Later, we'll tie them to the picket line. Supplement the grass with grain and hay pellets. They burn a lot of calories on these trips."

His care for the animals was obvious. More telling was how all the horses trusted and respected him. And when Brownie lowered his head against Bear's chest, he chuckled and scratched the horse's jaw. "My wife bred and raised this fellow. She'll only let me use him if his rider is a woman. Says he prefers a lighter touch."

Bear straightened, his breath beginning to mist in the cooling air. He turned to address the rest of the group, his voice carrying across the meadow. "Now let's get the tents pitched before we lose this light. We'll want everything secure before the temperature drops.

"Keep your rifles and saddlebags in your tents where they're secure." He gestured toward a pole attached chest-height between two thick pines. "Saddles and tack go on the saddle rack. We have a tarp to keep them dry and safe from porcupines. Those critters will chew anything salty, especially leather that's soaked up horse sweat."

The thought of porcupines munching on their saddles made everyone hurry to secure their gear. Then they turned to setting up camp, Bear carefully positioning each tent to ensure drainage and wind protection while keeping a view of the horses' tether line. His experience showed in how he chose the flattest ground for sleeping areas and positioned door flaps away from the prevailing wind.

The thunk of hammers driving stakes into the ground echoed off the surrounding cliffs, mixed with the rustle of nylon as they adjusted tent flies and stretched guy lines. The temperature kept dropping as the sun lowered, and Nikki was grateful for the windbreak provided by the trees.

She was also relieved to see they all had their own sleeping quarters and that her tent was to the left of Bear's, with the other three tents on his right. Whether intentional or not, the positioning provided both privacy and security.

The last light was fading from the peaks by the time she had her sleeping bag and belongings arranged in her tent. She joined Marcus and Doug in gathering small sticks to serve as kindling for the fire. Previous clients had picked the area close to camp clean, so she had to walk further out to find fallen twigs.

Gunner accompanied her, exploring the area and delighting in the freedom. But he suddenly sat, tail thumping, his signal that he'd found a familiar scent. She crouched down, but the rocky soil held few impressions and the light was fading. Still, she could depend on her dog's nose. And now she had confirmation that their watchers were the activists from earlier. Not random hikers.

"Good dog," she said, patting and praising him in lieu of his usual ball reward. Knowing that he would react consistently to the activists' presence was reassuring.

She carried an armload of scavenged twigs back to the fire pit where Bear was setting larger logs taken from his precious wood stash. She caught his eye and gave a subtle nod toward the trees, letting him decide whether to tell the others about their visitors.

Marcus's earlier comment about driving the intruders away bothered her. There'd been something in the man's tone that suggested he wasn't planning to rely on polite conversation.

Bear snapped a stick in half, the sharp crack the only sign that he understood her warning. He concentrated on arranging the kindling, building a pyramid of twigs and dry bark. When he touched a match to the tinder, the flames quickly caught, crackling and popping as they spread through the larger wood.

Soon the fire was throwing a healthy flame, its heat pushing back the mountain cold. The scent of burning pine mixed with wood smoke created a distinctive campfire smell that reminded her of evenings with Justin in the Sierra Nevada, where they'd sit by the fire planning their next day's ride. As darkness fell here too, the campfire became the center of their world, its dancing light playing across their faces, casting shadows beyond the circle of warmth.

"Now this is what I've been waiting for," Marcus said, settling on the log and producing a distinctive square bottle of whisky. "No drinking before or during the hunt, but tonight we can indulge."

Even in the flickering light, Nikki could see the elegant label that suggested this wasn't the kind of bottle you'd find at a convenience store.

Ryan grinned, accepting a splash in his tin cup. "To another bumpy trip stuck on a horse's back."

Even Doug smiled as he raised his cup. "Worth every sore muscle."

Bear waved off the offered drink, concentrating on setting a grill over hot coals. Nikki also declined, noting how the three men relaxed more with every sip. The alcohol was loosening tongues, and if she was lucky, the conversation might turn to Elena.

Bear stepped away from the fire then returned with two cans of low-alcohol beer, offering one to Nikki with a discreet wink. "Thought you might prefer this to Marcus's whisky," he said, his tone suggesting he'd picked up on her need to stay alert.

She took a grateful sip, appreciating both the beverage and his thoughtfulness. "How did you keep it so cold?" she asked, curious about his camping tricks.

"Made an enclosure of rocks and mesh, a natural refrigeration system that my youngest daughter designed," Bear said, gesturing toward the stream. "Keeps everything chilled."

The pride in his voice was obvious and Nikki raised her can in appreciation of his daughter's ingenuity. Coolers were too bulky to pack in on a horse and ice didn't last long. Having the ability to prolong the life of food on a week-long trip was an unexpected luxury. "How old is your daughter?"

"Fifteen. Both my kids work with me during the summer. My son's seventeen and helps with fishing clients. He prefers those trips over hunting."

Nikki fingered the cold can, knowing now that her tent placement hadn't been accidental. Bear understood a woman's concerns about camping with strange men. She found herself respecting him even more, and leaned back against the log, pleasantly tired as she enjoyed her cold beer and watched Bear tend to the sizzling steaks.

Soon wisps of aromatic smoke rose in the air, making her stomach growl with anticipation. Fat dripped into the ashes, causing brief flares that illuminated the eager faces. As their meal cooked, the group settled into the timeless rhythm of campfire evenings. Voices grew quieter, movements slower, the day's tensions easing as the flickering firelight worked its ancient magic.

Once everything was ready, Bear set the food on metal plates, added a scoop of hot baked beans, and passed them to the hungry riders. "Enjoy," he said. "After tonight it's more basic."

"Yeah," Marcus said, cutting into his steak. "Even if we shoot a deer early, we'd have to hang it to age. And cleaning and skinning is a lot of work. We sure don't want to return early." His gaze found Doug's. "I'd rather save my tag until the end of the week and hold out for a trophy buck. If I don't get one by then, I'll settle for something smaller."

Their conversation revealed more about their backgrounds as the evening progressed. Ryan was a geologist, like his father, and Doug was a lawyer in a large firm. Marcus was a successful financier, perhaps explaining his tendency to take charge and his expectation that others would defer to his judgment.

"We've been taking trips together since college," Marcus said. "Twenty-three years of friendship. Not many groups stay this tight."

"It helps that we love getting away," Ryan said with a chuckle. "Although I'm more comfortable looking at rocks than riding a horse."

They asked Nikki a few polite questions, seeming to assume from Bear's earlier introduction that she was employed by his insurance company. She didn't correct them, and none of them showed particular interest in Gunner beyond casual comments that he was well trained.

But Marcus kept returning to the subject of their uninvited visitors.

"You sure there's nothing we can do about those people?" he asked Bear for the third time. "I mean, if they're activists trying to disrupt our hunting, that has to be illegal."

"We need to catch them doing something specific," Bear replied. "I'd rather just keep an eye on them than go looking for trouble."

"Well, I think it's unacceptable," Marcus said. "We're paying premium rates for an exclusive experience."

Nikki pressed against the log, irritated with his persistence. Any hunter would be disappointed by unexpected company, but Marcus seemed obsessed. More notably, he didn't ask Doug's opinion. And Doug was the lawyer who would know about legal options.

The conversation died as the fire burned down, its flames no longer leaping but settling into a glowing bed of embers. She pulled her jacket tighter as the mountain cold inched closer.

Night sounds also became more noticeable. The hoot of an owl, wind sighing through the trees, and the rustle of rodents moving through the underbrush. Above them, stars appeared one by one, and the crescent moon hung like a silver blade, providing enough light to outline the peaks but leaving the valley in shadows.

Bear stood and stretched, breaking the spell that had settled over the group. "Time to bring the horses in. I've had animals that could travel five miles even with hobbles. No fun walking out if they get homesick."

They left the dying embers and spread out across the meadow to collect the scattered horses, who lifted their heads reluctantly from the grass, clearly content. After leading them to the stream for a final drink, the thud of hooves on grass created a peaceful backdrop as they walked toward the picket line.

Brownie behaved like a gentleman, seeming to understand the evening routine and walking calmly beside Nikki.

Bear rationed out pellets and grain from his cache. Nikki waited until Brownie had finished eating before tightening his rope. Then Bear moved along the line of horses checking the knots and making sure the ropes were a safe length.

The other three men had already returned to the campfire but she elected not to join them and called good night. Behind her, Bear lingered, giving each horse a good night pat, thanking them for their hard work.

She unzipped her tent flap, the sound harsh against the quiet. The interior was surprisingly spacious, with lots of room for her saddlebags. Light from the stars shone through the ventilation flaps, making it easy to arrange her sleeping bag and pad. Gunner followed her in, circling twice before curling up between her feet and the door.

Outside, the conversation around the fire was winding down. She heard Bear head toward his tent but not before warning the three men not to burn any more wood. The voices lowered but she could still pick up a few words. Something about market opportunity and the urgency of buying stock. She guessed Marcus never stopped selling, even on a hunting trip with his friends.

She shifted, trying to get comfortable. Despite the pad beneath her sleeping bag, a sharp rock pressed into her hip. She rolled onto her back, reviewing the day's discoveries: the activists and their dangerous tripline, Marcus's aversion to visitors, Bear's competence.

She thought she was too wired to sleep but she must have dozed off as the next thing she heard was Gunner's low growl. She lay motionless, listening, every sense jolted alert. He growled again, a definite warning. She eased out of her sleeping bag and crawled to the door. Slowly raised the zipper, remembering its earlier noise.

The picket line was visible beneath the moonlight. Scout's gray hindquarters stood out while the other horses were dark shapes. But they were restless, shifting sideways and snorting. At first she thought an animal had disturbed them, then she caught movement by Scout's head. Two figures with arms raised.

Dammit. They were untying the lead ropes.

"Hey!" she called, rolling out from the tent so fast she almost fell. "Get away from there. We have an attack dog."

But she kept a firm grip on Gunner's collar. No way was she letting him race up to hostile intruders who might be armed with knives or guns.

At least her warning worked. The figures bolted, melting into the darkness. Within seconds, Bear emerged from his tent, rifle in his hands.

"What happened?" he asked.

"Two people around the horses," Nikki said, following as he hurried toward the picket line.

Brownie and Scout were loose, grabbing snatches of grass as they wandered toward the meadow, delighted with their unexpected freedom. But they both stopped when Bear said "whoa." He retied them, checked the other knots, then nodded at Gunner. "Never thought I'd say this, but I'm glad you brought your dog. He's better than any alarm system."

"I'm not too worried about loose horses," Bear went on. "None of these guys are the type to bolt for home. The activists probably figured that out after watching Brownie and Scout stop to eat grass. It's the other things they might try that worry me. Cut cinches, spook them with noisemakers, even put something in their feed. An injured horse this far from help..." He didn't finish the thought, but his meaning was clear.

Nikki shivered as she stared at the dark trees. The tripwire had been telling. If the activists were willing to string that across a trail, they didn't care about hurting innocent animals. The thought of a horse stumbling off a cliff because of sabotage was horrifying. Whatever game they were playing, it was escalating beyond simple harassment. And with Elena's death still unexplained, she couldn't shake the fear that this might all be connected.

CHAPTER EIGHT

When Nikki crawled from her tent the next morning, the sun was rising over the eastern peaks, painting the cliffs in shades of gold. Frost glittered on the grass, and her breath misted. She tightened her jacket, feeling the bite on her face. Bear was already up, moving around the fire pit. The other three tents remained zippered, tight and silent.

"Those guys are always lazy on their first morning," he said with a chuckle, gesturing toward the men's tents. "Ryan especially. He barely even rides." Bear spoke with the bewilderment of one who never walked when he could ride, and couldn't understand anyone not feeling the same way.

While they waited for the camp to stir, Nikki helped Bear grain the animals and check them over for any cuts or swellings.

"You're good with horses," Bear said. "Once I show you the lay of the land, you're cleared to ride by yourself. Marcus and Doug do that as well." He glanced toward Ryan's tent. "Ryan still needs either me or one of his friends with him. He's improved over the years, but not enough to be trusted alone."

They led the horses to the stream in small groups, the animals drinking deeply from the clear water. The morning was so peaceful that every sound seemed amplified: the splash of a jumping fish, the dripping from a horse's muzzle, the call of a circling red-tailed hawk. Somewhere in the fir grove, a woodpecker hammered against dead bark, the rapid drumming cutting the air.

When Brownie finished drinking, he lifted his head and stared at the bottom of the cliff. A flat shelf, carpeted with grass, stretched in front of the granite wall. The natural corridor looked like it had been designed for riding, protected from wind and offering stunning views.

"It looks like nice riding over there," Nikki said, following Brownie's gaze, wondering what had grabbed the horse's attention.

"Yes, it's nice and flat. The deer like it too. But avoid the cliffs. Some of those higher trails are barely wide enough for a horse." Bear's expression darkened. "Including the ridge where Elena fell. Nobody should ride that trail alone."

"Why was she there?"

Bear gave his head a slow shake. "That's the million-dollar question. And one the police kept asking me. Earlier that week she was talking about checking on some plant species. Used some Latin names I didn't know. She and Doug had a conversation about water quality but we were all doing our own thing. I don't understand why she went up there. Believe me, she'd been warned."

Bear's voice carried a weight of regret. "Come on," he said, turning away. "Let's get these guys to the meadow so they have time to eat before saddling."

The conversation was over, but his emotion was evident as they hobbled the horses and left them to graze. Nikki sympathized with Bear. He was clearly carrying a heavy burden about Elena's death. But she felt worse for the dead woman and her grieving husband. Questions needed to be asked, no matter how uncomfortable they left the guide.

She returned to her tent and pulled out Gunner's kibble and travel bowl. He ate with gusto. Though he clearly considered this a fun vacation, the long hike yesterday had left him with an appetite.

When he'd licked his bowl clean, she clipped on his leash and led him to the picket line, letting him check out the tracks from last night's visitors. His reaction was obvious, confirming that it was the same group. She turned toward the cliff face, wondering if they were hiding up there, watching through binoculars.

Part of her admired their tenacity. They'd hiked into this remote area, carrying minimal supplies, driven by conviction. But passion for a cause could also create zealots who justified extreme actions. Peaceful protesters could escalate to violence, convinced that righteousness excused any means necessary. Leaders like Derek Stone were skilled at transforming idealists into dangerous fanatics.

The thought chilled her and she suddenly wanted a hot cup of coffee as well as the company of others. By the time she walked back to the camp circle, Marcus had joined Bear and was sipping from a steaming mug. Even this early, he looked well groomed, as if ready for a board meeting rather than a day in the wilderness.

"Did you hear our visitors last night?" Bear asked Marcus. "They tried to untie our horses."

"Damn!" Marcus wheeled, staring in the direction of the horses, relaxing when he saw all seven were still there. "I didn't hear a thing. Glad you took care of it. Nobody wants to walk all those miles back to the trailhead."

"I didn't do anything. Nikki's dog ran them off."

"Wish I'd intercepted them. I'd put an end to this harassment." He fixed Bear with a pointed stare. "You still planning to contact the Forest Service once their office opens?"

"Absolutely," Bear said. "That wire trap could have hurt someone."

"But it seems like we're inviting more interference," Marcus said, his voice taking on an edge. "I think it's better to handle things ourselves."

Bear poured Nikki a cup of coffee, the pot clanking against her metal cup with more force than necessary. He began setting out plates, each metallic clatter emphasizing his displeasure. The silence stretched as Marcus waited for a response that didn't come. Bear's movements became increasingly sharp, making it clear he didn't appreciate having his decisions questioned, especially by a client.

"I'll be riding to the ridge with Nikki today," Bear finally said. "Just the two of us."

Marcus gave a little nod, as if Bear had been asking for his approval. "Good idea. Show her the boundaries. Doug and Ryan can scout around but I'll stay in camp and keep an eye on the pack horses. Make sure those activists don't try anything."

Nikki found his word choice odd. Boundaries implied territorial limits that needed to be respected, but this was public wilderness where anyone could legally hike or ride. He spoke as if he had some claim to the land beyond their temporary hunting permits. And his suggestion about handling things themselves carried an undertone that left her uneasy. Handle how?

The sound of a tent zipper interrupted her thoughts. Doug emerged, zipping his tent shut behind him. He carried a sleek spotting scope, handling it with the care of someone who'd invested serious money in the equipment.

"New scope?" Bear asked, his eyes widening with appreciation. "Looks like a good one."

"Been waiting all summer to try this out," Doug said, his voice unusually animated. "Supposed to be the best for long-range spotting."

"We use the spot-and-stalk approach," Bear said, turning to Nikki. "No tree stands. More sporting to find the deer, then figure out how to get close enough for a clean shot."

"Stalking is the most fun," Doug said. "Patience, reading the terrain, moving without being detected. You have to think like your prey, anticipate their every move." His voice grew more animated. "There's nothing like the thrill of following their trail, getting closer and closer until you're close enough to shoot. It's the ultimate game of predator and prey."

The way he spoke sent a chill down Nikki's neck. There was something unsettling about his enthusiasm for hunting animals that couldn't fight back, his pleasure in the psychological aspects of the hunt.

She took a quick sip of coffee, grabbing the chance to break eye contact. The sound of Ryan shuffling from his tent gave her another reason to look away. His cheerful greeting was a relief after Doug's intensity.

Ryan had his equipment bag tucked beneath an arm, the same black bag he'd coaxed Bear into packing. He looked excited and ready for the day although he was dressed more like a geologist than a hunter. His khaki field pants had multiple cargo pockets, his sheepskin vest had loops and clips for tools. Even his boots were the sturdy hiking type favored by scientists.

"Great to wake up on the mountain," he said, still grinning as he accepted coffee from Bear. "My grandfather used to bring me here when I was a kid. My dad too. They were fascinated with the geology. The way the limestone metamorphosed into marble, all those mineral intrusions from volcanic activity. Creates unique formations."

"They both came here?" Bear asked, slicing cheese and setting out a variety of smoked meat. "That was wild country back then. Your dad probably has some good stories."

Ryan's smile faded. "My father died a couple years ago. But he talked about the deposits, the formations—"

Marcus reached out and squeezed Ryan's shoulder. "No need to rehash sad times. You're on vacation."

"Right," Ryan said, color spotting his cheeks. "Sorry, no more talk of that."

An awkward silence followed but Nikki thought Marcus had been rather hard on his friend. And Ryan's stories probably wouldn't be boring. Her research before the trip had mentioned old copper mining claims, though most had been abandoned decades ago when the ore played out. The formations Ryan mentioned would explain why miners had been drawn here in the first place.

She turned toward him, intending to ask a few more questions but Marcus and Ryan had already moved on to a different topic. And Bear had finished toasting thick buns that left her mouth watering.

"Buns don't squash in packs like regular bread," he explained as he assembled open-face sandwiches and passed out the laden plates.

Nikki bit into her breakfast. The combination of crispy bread, melted cheese, and smoky meat was surprisingly delicious, and she gave Bear a grateful smile.

"Trail cooking is an essential skill," Bear said. "We have to make the most out of simple ingredients."

She ate quickly, deciding that Bear could be a chef if his guide business didn't work out. But she doubted he'd want to hear that. And there'd be plenty of time to talk when they were riding this morning.

Away from the group, she'd be able to ask some pointed questions about Elena's death. The insurance company was paying her to get answers, and she couldn't do that effectively with Marcus and the others listening. She needed Bear's honest assessment of what had happened on that ridge, without the filter of client relations or the pressure of maintaining his reputation.

Twenty minutes later, she and Bear were saddling their horses while the three men washed the dishes. If they were annoyed she was monopolizing their guide for a few hours, they hid it well.

Brownie stood patiently while she tightened the cinch, though he kept looking at his buddies as if wishing he could stay and eat grass. Following Bear's instructions, she kept the halter on beneath his bridle and also packed hobbles and a lead rope.

"Always carry them," Bear had told her. "If you need to scout on foot, you don't want your horse wandering away. The halter means you can let him graze just by slipping off the bridle." His expression grew more serious. "And you never know when you might have to tie your horse. Best to be prepared."

Taking his advice, Nikki had packed light in her tent that morning. Her saddlebags contained only the essentials: hobbles, lead rope, water, Gunner's items, pepper spray, cell phone for taking pictures, protein bars and her Glock. Lastly she buckled on her dog's safety vest, remembering the zeal in Doug's eyes when he spoke about stalking prey. She didn't want anyone mistaking Gunner for a deer.

"Ready?" Bear asked, as he swung into the saddle.

Nikki nodded and mounted, settling into the familiar rhythm of Brownie's energetic walk. Behind them, the camp was already taking on the look of clients pursuing different agendas: Marcus finishing the dish washing, Doug assembling his spotting scope, and Ryan eagerly checking the contents of his black bag.

The three friends were so different. Marcus the commanding financier, Doug the methodical lawyer, Ryan the easygoing geologist. The fact that they'd remained close for over twenty years was impressive. But there were rifts. The way Marcus silenced Ryan, how Doug and Ryan deferred to his leadership, the odd looks they exchanged when certain topics came up. Whatever bound them together went deeper than college friendship.

But those secrets were unimportant. Elena Vasquez's death was Nikki's priority. The trail where the researcher had taken her final breath lay ahead. Something had drawn the woman to that dangerous ridge, something worth risking her life. And Nikki needed to find the reason.

CHAPTER NINE

The granite cliff towered above them as Nikki and Bear rode along its base, their horses' hooves striking the rocky ground with metallic rings. Morning shadows clung to the cliff face, creating a cool corridor.

Bear pointed toward a series of narrow cuts zigzagging up the steep rock face. "Game trails," he said, his voice carrying in the still air. "Deer and elk use them, but they're way too steep for horses. Even experienced hikers think twice before tackling those routes."

Nikki studied the treacherous paths, some barely wider than a footprint, others disappearing entirely where the granite became too sheer. A few scraggly manzanita bushes clung to cracks in the rock, their red bark bright against the gray stone.

"Elena fell from one of those?" she asked. The thought of plummeting through empty air, scrambling desperately for any handhold as granite walls rushed past, only to crash onto the jagged rocks below, left her nauseous. A fall from that height would leave no hope of survival.

"Higher up. There's a ridge trail that connects to these game paths." Bear's expression darkened. "Should have been marked dangerous years ago. But the Forest Service is always short-staffed."

They continued along the bottom of the cliff, Gunner trotting beside them, his orange vest a splash of color against the muted autumn landscape. A red squirrel chattered at them from a white bark pine, and somewhere above, the harsh cry of a crow echoed off the granite walls.

After another mile, Bear reined his buckskin toward a wider trail that switchbacked up the mountainside. "This is the main route," he said. "Built for pack animals when the mining claims were active. Good footing all the way to the ridge."

The trail was indeed well-constructed, carved into the slope with proper drainage and graded turns that allowed the horses to climb easily. Nikki relaxed in the saddle, able to look around rather than focus on the footing.

The sparse landscape contrasted with what it must have been like during Elena's spring trip. A few hardy asters showed purple blooms, and the occasional clump of rabbit brush added yellow color, but most of the flowers had long since gone to seed.

"What would Elena have found here in May?" Nikki asked, scanning the trail edges for any sign of the woman's missing cameras.

"A completely different world." Bear's voice warmed with enthusiasm. "Indian paintbrush everywhere, lupine covering whole hillsides. Mountain lilies along the stream corridors, and the butterflies. Incredible migrations coming through. Elena seemed interested in the pollinators, how the bees and butterflies moved between elevations as different flowers bloomed."

Nikki nodded, imagining the spring abundance while continuing to scan for the biologist's trail cams. The devices were small, designed to blend with bark and rock, but surely she could spot one. Unless someone else had grabbed them first.

The sound of water grew louder as they climbed, and soon they reached a small waterfall cascading down the cliff face. It sluiced through a narrow chute in the granite before pooling in natural basins carved by centuries of flow. The water continued downhill in a series of small cascades, disappearing into the forest below.

"Beautiful," Nikki said, watching the play of sunlight on the water. Then she remembered something Bear had said. "You mentioned Elena discussed water quality with Doug. Do you remember anything specific?"

Bear's shoulders sagged and he fiddled with his horse's mane before looking at her. "I was cleaning up after dinner, not really listening. They were looking at some sort of testing kit, talking about pH levels or something scientific. Doug seemed interested, but you know how it is around a campfire. Lots of different conversations going on."

"Did the police ask Doug any questions?"

"Don't know," Bear said. "They certainly talked to me. Wanted to know her route that morning, whether she'd mentioned where she was going. The whole thing was treated as a riding accident. And frankly I was happy about that."

Nikki's mouth tightened. Another angle the investigation had missed, another potential lead that hadn't been followed. She was beginning to think Elena's death deserved much closer scrutiny than it had received.

They continued climbing, the trail crisscrossing back and forth. Ponderosa pines provided occasional shade, their vanilla-scented bark warming in the sun. Gunner kept his easy jog alongside the horses, clearly enjoying the trail's moderate grade and the variety of scents. He suddenly stopped and sat, his ears pricked as he looked up at Nikki.

"Probably just picked up a deer," Bear said, noting Gunner's posture. "Or maybe a coyote."

"No, this is different." Nikki studied her dog's body language, recognizing the signs that told her he'd identified a familiar scent. "He's alerting to a human."

Bear lifted a skeptical eyebrow."We're pretty far from anywhere. Who would he smell up here?"

"The activists from last night. He had a strong scent from when they were messing with the horses. If you don't mind a detour, I'd like to check it out. Maybe we can smooth things out with them." Without Marcus around waving a gun.

Bear glanced up at the sun. "We should have time. Best to try talking before this escalates into something worse. And I have to admit, I'm curious about where they're camped."

Gunner led them off the main trail onto what appeared to be another game path, this one winding through dense stands of Douglas fir and cedar. The going was slower here, the horses picking their way over fallen logs and around large boulders. But Gunner moved with growing confidence, his pace quickening.

They emerged into a small clearing tucked beneath towering trees. An olive-green tent sat nearly invisible against the forest backdrop, and a camouflaged tarp had been strung between several trees, creating additional shelter. Beneath the tarp, fishing rods and various belongings were scattered with the casual disorder of a long-term camp.

"Well hidden," Bear said softly. "Took some skill to find this spot. Perfect vantage point too. They can probably see our camp from here, monitor all our comings and goings. And without horses, steep terrain doesn't slow them."

The camp seemed deserted, but Nikki could see recent signs of habitation: fresh ashes in a small fire ring, damp clothing hanging from a line, and a hatchet stuck into a fallen log.

"Hello, the camp!" Bear called, following wilderness etiquette by announcing their presence.

Nothing stirred. Then rustling sounded from inside the tent, followed by urgent whispers. A man crawled out, tucking in his shirt and blinking in the filtered sunlight, He was followed by a woman who looked equally startled.

Nikki recognized the man. He was the same intense individual she'd seen in Derek Stone's office. He looked just as hardened and just as confident, even in his disheveled state. The woman was younger, maybe mid-twenties, with short-cropped blonde hair and the lean build of someone who spent time outdoors.

Both activists wore expressions of resentment as they took in their mounted visitors.

"Good morning," Bear said, politely touching the brim of his cowboy hat. "I'm Bear Hutchins. I guide hunting parties through this area, but I believe in everyone respecting each other's activities. Hope we can share these mountains peacefully."

"I'm Jake," the man said curtly. His eyes narrowed as he studied Bear, then shifted to glare at the horses. There was something hostile in his gaze, as if the horses were enemy combatants, as guilty as their riders.

Nikki instinctively reached out to touch Brownie's neck, guessing that this man would have no qualms about hurting her horse. But it was the woman's reaction that was even more bizarre. She jerked back, her eyes locked on Bear and his horse, with an expression akin to horror.

"These are public lands," Jake said, stepping in front of the woman. "But you people act like you own it. Just look at the damage you're causing."

He jabbed a thumb at the horses. "Their hooves are destroying delicate root systems. Their manure is introducing bacteria and parasites into pristine watersheds. They're eating native vegetation that wildlife depend on for survival."

His voice grew more heated. "And that hay and grain you feed them! It's loaded with foreign seeds that establish invasive species. You're literally destroying the ecosystem with every ride."

Bear remained calm, though Nikki noticed his buckskin beginning to fidget, sensing his rider's annoyance. "I understand your concerns," Bear said, his voice admirably level. "But horses have been part of this landscape for over a century. The mining operations, the Forest Service patrols, the search and rescue teams. They all use horses. Traditional use, protected by law."

His tone remained measured, showing no trace of anger even though he was speaking to someone who was trying to sabotage his business. It was the response of a man who seemed to accept that lasting solutions required dialogue, not confrontation.

"Traditional destruction," Jake snapped. "Just because something's been done for a long time doesn't make it right."

Bear gestured toward Nikki, clearly trying to defuse the situation. "This is Nikki Drake. She's not a hunter. She's here on insurance business, looking into a biologist's death that occurred this spring."

Nikki noted how the woman's face whitened beneath her tan. And something clicked.

"Are you Sage Crux?" Nikki asked. "I understand you found Elena's body. I'm sorry about what you experienced."

Sage nodded, but she barely looked at Nikki. She just stared at Bear, her hands twisting at the hem of her flannel shirt, as if caught in a terrible memory.

"Did you talk to Elena before her death?" Nikki asked gently. "Did she mention her research?"

"I talked to her," Sage said, her voice whisper thin. "But not for long."

Gunner moved closer, his tail wagging as he pressed his nose into Sage's hand. She automatically patted his head, the contact seeming to steady her. Still, her eyes never left Bear's face, filled with visceral fear that seemed to come from nowhere. Nikki found the reaction strange. She could tell from Bear's baffled expression that he'd never seen this woman before, yet Sage looked at him like he was her worst nightmare.

"Sage doesn't have to answer questions from you people." Jake swung toward the log and scooped up the hatchet in a lithe move, as if he knew exactly where he'd placed it. His muscles coiled as he turned to face them. "And we don't appreciate being spied on. Now I suggest you move along before someone else gets hurt."

Gunner's tail stopped wagging, his growl quick and low. Nikki called him back, away from that deadly hatchet, her mind still puzzling over Sage's odd reaction.

"No need for threats," Bear said. "We're just trying to have a conversation."

However, the peaceful morning had turned tense, charged with the type of hostility that could escalate. And Nikki's stomach churned with an unease that had nothing to do with the hatchet Jake was brandishing.

Because Sage's fear went beyond nervousness. The woman had recognized Bear, and her terror suggested something far worse than a disagreeable encounter. What if Sage had seen something that day on the ridge? What if Bear's helpful cooperation was actually the performance of someone with everything to hide?

Nikki forced herself to breathe, to appear relaxed as they turned their horses. But sweat gathered at the base of her neck, and every instinct urged her to put distance between them, to leave Bear and gallop back to camp where others would provide safety in numbers.

Instead, she had to continue this ride as if nothing had changed, all the while wondering if she was alone in the wilderness with Elena's killer.

CHAPTER TEN

The trail narrowed as they rode away from the activists' camp, forcing Nikki to follow. She found herself studying Bear's every move. The way he sat deep in his saddle, the hunting knife sheathed at his hip, the rifle secured in its leather scabbard. All tools of his trade, she reminded herself. Perfectly normal equipment for a wilderness guide.

But normal had taken on a sinister edge. Every creak of leather, every shift of his weight in the saddle seemed ominous. The way he adjusted his reins made her wonder if he was positioning himself for some sort of attack. Even his easy breathing seemed calculated, as if he was deliberately staying calm while planning his next move. When a branch snapped under his horse's hoof, she jerked in the saddle, her hand reaching back toward her right saddlebag. And her gun.

She straightened, reminding herself that Bear still viewed her as just an insurance investigator, hired by the company to rubber-stamp their findings. He had no idea she was a licensed PI. She tried to remember if he'd seen her loading her saddlebags yesterday morning. She didn't think he'd spotted her Glock, carefully wrapped and tucked beneath her extra clothes. And really, what reason would he have to hurt her? She was just an insurance investigator doing routine follow-up. Even if Bear was Elena's killer, the smart thing would be to cooperate, to appear helpful, and let her write a report concluding it was an accident.

Still, the landscape around them had lost its beauty, colors fading to muted browns and grays. Dead leaves rustled with the wind, their brittle whispers following her up the increasingly steep trail. The shadows were deeper here, the isolation more complete. If something happened in these remote mountains, it could be a long time before anyone found her body.

Bear seemed oblivious to her mounting tension, his attention focused elsewhere.

"That Jake character really bothers me," he said, glancing over his shoulder. "Did you see how fast he grabbed that hatchet? The guy's unhinged."

"He seemed angry," Nikki agreed, though she was more bothered by the image of Sage's terrified face when Bear had introduced himself.

"It's more than anger. These radical environmentalists think they're justified in any action. I've heard stories about activists poisoning water used by horses and we've already seen that tripwire." Bear's voice carried genuine concern. "They view us as the enemy, and some of them are capable of anything."

His worry for the horses seemed authentic, which only added to her confusion. Would a cold-blooded killer show such concern? Or was this just another layer of deception, designed to maintain his helpful guide persona?

"That woman, Sage, seemed frightened," Nikki said, watching Bear's shoulders, testing his reaction.

"Probably afraid of what Jake might do if she talked too much. He's clearly the one calling the shots."

But Nikki wasn't convinced. Sage's terror had been directed at Bear. Not Jake. And if Sage had simply found Elena's body as she'd told police, why the obvious fear? Unless Sage had seen something else, something she hadn't reported. Maybe she'd witnessed more than just the aftermath of an accident. Something that implicated Bear, something she'd discovered later that connected him to Elena's death. That might explain her fear.

Bear seemed oblivious to Nikki's suspicions, still focused on what he saw as the real threat. He continued grumbling about Jake as the trail wound through stands of fir with granite outcroppings becoming more frequent. Nikki made appropriate murmurs of agreement, letting Bear vent his frustrations while her mind centered on more pressing concerns.

She wished she could speak to Sage alone. The woman seemed to know something about Elena's death, something that left her terrified. But Jake had hovered over her like a protective guard dog, and they were camped in remote wilderness where private conversations would be nearly impossible. Even if Nikki could somehow separate Sage from Jake, the young woman seemed too frightened to speak.

Maybe it was time to contact the police and ask them to reopen Elena's case. A formal investigation might compel Sage to talk, and trained detectives would have resources Nikki lacked. But that would mean admitting her insurance investigation had uncovered potential evidence of murder. A conclusion that could destroy Bear's livelihood if she were wrong.

The weight of that responsibility sat heavy on her shoulders as they continued their climb. After another half hour, Bear reined his horse toward a small meadow tucked beneath towering granite walls. The grass here was still green despite the season, fed by moisture seeping from cracks in the rock above.

"This is where that Sage woman claims she found Brownie," Bear said, dismounting near a cluster of bushes. His tone carried a note of skepticism. "Poor horse was just grazing here, reins supposedly dragging. My horses are trained to ground tie, so he wouldn't have wandered far. But I've always wondered what that activist was really doing here when she 'found' him."

He made air quotes around the word 'found,' his expression suggesting he had doubts about Sage's version of events.

Nikki swung down from her saddle, giving a nod while concealing her own concerns. She pulled her phone from the saddlebag and slipped her pepper spray into her jacket pocket. The spray wasn't much protection against Bear's rifle, but it might buy precious seconds. She forced herself to follow his pointing arm, trying to focus on the investigation.

"They think Elena went over just to the left of that marble," Bear said. "Judging by the location of her body."

Nikki stared up at the towering cliff face where a distinctive white streak ran through the gray granite. It had to be a hundred-foot drop.

The cliff was almost vertical, offering no handholds or ledges that might break a fall. Jagged boulders littered the base, some as large as cars, creating an unforgiving landing. The brutal terrain made the written accident report seem inadequate. No description could convey the hopelessness of that fall.

But as Nikki swallowed back the lump in her throat, one detail struck her as crucial. Brownie stood beside her, grazing contentedly on the grass. No signs of fear, no nervous energy.

Horses had excellent memories, especially for traumatic events. And it didn't appear that Brownie had been involved in Elena's fall. He hadn't spooked, sending the woman to her death. And he certainly hadn't fallen. No horse could have survived the drop.

"So we agree Elena was on foot when she went over," Nikki said, watching Bear's reaction.

He nodded, but his expression was bitter. "But that's not what the insurance company wants you to prove, is it? They want to hear that I sent her on an unsuitable horse, let her ride on a dangerous ridge."

Nikki couldn't deny that truth. Insurance companies made money by finding reasons not to pay claims, and negligence on Bear's part would be the perfect excuse. "You're right," she admitted. "They'd much rather find liability than pay out a large settlement. What exactly would your insurance cover?"

"It's covered as an accidental death either way. But if they can prove guide negligence, then they'll sue my liability insurance to recover what they paid out. And then drop me as a client because I'm too high risk. No insurance means no guiding business."

The cynicism in his voice was understandable, matching what Nikki knew about insurance companies and their creative approaches to avoiding payouts. But it also gave Bear a clear motive for wanting Elena's death ruled accidental rather than the result of his poor judgment.

"Did the police examine the ledge?" Nikki asked.

"No, they just took my statement and called it an accident. Seemed obvious enough. Woman falls off cliff, woman dies. They didn't see any need to climb up there and investigate." Bear gestured toward the steep face. "Can't say I blame them. The outcome was pretty clear."

Nikki sighed, staring up at the white marble streak, knowing she needed to see that ledge. Whatever had happened up there, the answers weren't going to be found at the bottom.

"Let's unsaddle the horses and give them a break," she said. "Then I'd like to climb up and see where Elena fell."

Bear looked surprised. "The insurance company wants you to go up there?"

"They want a thorough investigation," Nikki said, checking her phone for a signal. No bars, as expected, but plenty of battery. She switched to camera mode and snapped some pictures of the cliff as well as the grazing Brownie. "And I can't write a complete report without examining the scene."

"Your call. The climb's not too bad, and there's only one spot where it's really narrow. We can stop before that." He gave her a conspiratorial wink. "Can't have you reporting that I was negligent in taking you out on a ledge. I need this insurance thing to go away, and you understand how these companies work."

He seemed to consider her an ally, which eased her concern. If Bear saw her as someone ready to clear him with the insurance company, he was unlikely to view her as a threat. More importantly, he didn't seem to realize she'd picked up on Sage's terrified reaction. As far as Bear knew, their encounter with the activists had been nothing more than a brief confrontation with troublemakers. He had no clue that she was now questioning whether he'd been personally involved in Elena's death.

They worked in companionable silence, removing saddles and bridles before hobbling both horses so they could graze. Bear even helped her adjust Brownie's hobbles, his movements relaxed and unhurried, clearly assuming that she was on his side.

Gunner lapped at the trickling water then investigated the meadow, entranced by all the new scents. He lingered over a particularly interesting trail, hackles rising as he sniffed the ground.

Nikki noted his behavior. She'd never seen him react that way to an animal scent. Whatever he'd found was definitely predatory. His posture suggested something large and potentially dangerous, but not human.

"What's he found?" Bear asked, watching Gunner with the attention of someone who understood animal behavior.

"Something unusual. He's trying to catalog a scent. Something he's not used to. Maybe a bear?"

"Maybe," Bear said, though he sounded as doubtful as Nikki. "This is prime time for bears. But I would have expected that we crossed their scent yesterday. And he didn't react like that. Cougar maybe?"

"That would explain why he's so interested. They're not so common where we're from."

"They're active this time of year," Bear said, "following the deer herds as they move to winter range. If one's been hunting in the adjoining valley, it might use the ridge as a travel route. Better keep Gunner behind you when we get closer to the ledge."

Nikki nodded. Whatever had left that trail was somewhere in these mountains, and Gunner's behavior showed it deserved caution. Bear's concern about the unknown predator eased some of her suspicions about his involvement with Elena's death. A man planning harm wouldn't be so focused on potential wildlife threats, though she reminded herself that Bear might be more complex than he appeared.

She pulled Gunner's leash from the saddlebag before they started up the mountain, clipping it to his collar. She didn't want him charging ahead and confronting whatever predator had left that scent. His protective instincts were admirable, but they could get him killed if he felt obligated to take on a cougar or bear.

And he could provoke a wild animal into attacking when it might have retreated. Dogs had a way of triggering predatory responses, their barking and aggressive postures escalating situations that calm humans could defuse. The last thing they needed was to turn a routine climb into a life-or-death struggle.

With Gunner safe on his leash beside her, Nikki followed Bear up the winding path. The trail grew steeper as they climbed and the scent of pine mixed with the smell of sun-warmed stone. Loose pebbles skittered beneath their feet, bouncing and clattering down, marking the growing distance to the bottom.

She found herself breathing harder despite her and Justin's conditioning program. Below, the meadow had shrunk to a small patch of green, the grazing horses visible but reduced to toylike figures. Their bright orange halters stood out, unmistakable signals to any hunter that they weren't wild animals.

After ten more minutes of steady climbing, they reached the ridge. Nikki gasped, captivated by the view. Another valley spread below the far side of the cliff, carpeted with pristine timber and dotted with small meadows. No roads, no trails, no sign of human presence. Just pure wilderness.

"Beautiful, isn't it?" Bear said, noting her expression. "Virgin timber, native grasslands. That valley probably hasn't changed in centuries. It's inaccessible to hunters. Too narrow to bring pack horses up here so no way to get meat out even if we shot something."

He gestured ahead where the trail continued along the granite spine. The ridge path wasn't as narrow as she'd feared, though it was certainly treacherous. She and Gunner had traveled over much worse terrain, but that had been when lives were at stake. She wasn't about to risk her partner's safety for no reason.

She motioned for him to stay as the trail thinned and the white marble cut through the rock like a scar. That was where Elena had fallen. Nikki and Bear both stood silent, sobered by standing in the fatal spot.

She pulled out her phone, surprised to see there was now a signal bar. The elevation and lack of obstruction must have provided enough coverage to connect to a distant cell tower. But as she snapped pictures of the ledge, and its absence of scratches left by horseshoes, her questions multiplied.

The trail was narrow but not impossibly so. An experienced researcher like Elena, someone accustomed to remote fieldwork, should have been able to navigate it safely, especially on foot. Had the woman come here seeking cell coverage, perhaps to report her findings? She might have known about this signal spot. According to the police report, Sage had climbed higher to call 911 after finding Elena's body. This could be the same area where she'd made that emergency call.

But that still didn't explain what had gone wrong. Had Elena slipped while distracted by her phone? Been startled by wildlife? Or had someone else been on this ledge with her—someone who knew she'd come here looking for a signal?

Nikki stared down at the brutal drop, knowing the answers lay in understanding why Elena had risked this climb. Whether it was for cell coverage, research purposes, or because someone had lured her here, the truth was hidden somewhere in her final days.

Nikki would have to keep digging. Because the only thing she'd learned today was that Brownie wasn't involved. And that for some reason Sage was deathly afraid of Bear.

CHAPTER ELEVEN

Welcoming nickers met Nikki and Bear when they returned to camp. Brownie lengthened his stride, equally happy to be home. Only three horses were visible: the two pack horses and Marcus's bay gelding but all three lifted their heads from the grass to greet their returning friends.

Marcus stepped out from the trees at the edge of the meadow, clearly taking his guard duties seriously. He straightened his shirt and ran fingers through his hair as he approached. He looked happy to see them, although not quite as enthusiastic as the horses. Still, there was a restless energy in his long stride. No doubt he'd been bored on his own.

"How'd it go?" he asked, moving to help with the horses. "Find anything interesting up there?"

Bear swung down from his buckskin and began loosening the cinch. "Routine stuff. Nikki got her insurance photos, saw the scene." He glanced at Nikki as she dismounted. "Met some activists. Nothing too exciting."

Marcus reached out to pat Gunner, but the dog swerved around his hand, choosing instead to sniff at the base of a tree. The snub was subtle but deliberate, and Nikki noted how Marcus's mouth flattened. No doubt he wasn't used to rejection.

"So you found them," Marcus said, turning back toward Bear. "Where are they camped? How many?"

"Only two," Bear replied, pulling the saddle from his horse and setting it on the chest-high tack log. "Hidden in the timber. They're actually camped on the ridge just above us. As the crow flies, they're very close."

"So they can see everything we do?" Marcus scowled. "Did they say how long they're planning to stay? What kind of supplies are they carrying?"

Bear looked up from brushing sweat marks off his horse's back. "They didn't exactly invite us for breakfast, Marcus. But they seemed settled in for a while."

Nikki noted how Marcus's questions seemed more purposeful than polite. He wasn't just making small talk. She placed Brownie's saddle on the rack and began working the brush over his chest, keeping her movements casual while trying to listen.

"Speaking of dinner," Bear said, "where are Doug and Ryan? They should be back by now."

"Still out spotting game." Marcus gave a dismissive shrug. "Doug was excited to try out his standalone scope. Said they'd be gone most of the day."

Bear nodded, pulling hobbles from his saddlebags and looping them over his shoulder. "As long as they're together and staying on the lower trails. And no one shoots anything without me. We need to make sure the game is retrievable."

"Doug didn't even take his rifle," Marcus said. "Just wanted to scout around. Use his new scope to see what's out there."

Bear seemed satisfied with this explanation, but Marcus's tone carried the ease of someone accustomed to managing information, deciding what others needed to know. It struck Nikki as odd that Marcus and Doug, the most avid hunters of the group, hadn't asked

Ryan to stay behind and watch camp. Ryan was more interested in the wilderness experience than shooting a deer, and he probably wouldn't have minded being assigned guard duty.

The thought nagged at her as she and Bear finished grooming their horses and led them out to the meadow. Marcus trailed behind, his restless energy suggesting he had something on his mind.

Bear retrieved a compact case from his saddlebags and pulled out a satellite phone.

"You're still going to report that wire?" Marcus asked. "Seems like we might be overreacting. Those activists will probably relocate once they realize their tactics aren't working. No need to turn this into a federal matter."

Bear ignored Marcus, powering up the device and checking the signal strength. "Tripwires that can cripple horses aren't something to ignore," he finally said. "Right now I'm the only guide operating in this area. But if someone else uses that trail, they might not be so lucky." He turned his attention back to getting a clear satellite connection.

"We could take turns keeping watch," Marcus said, his voice turning persuasive. "Like I did today."

"The Forest Service needs to know. This is their land, their responsibility."

"Fine," Marcus said, although his clipped tone showed he didn't think it was fine at all. "But if you get a connection, may I call my office? Just a quick check in."

"Nope." Bear looked up, as if surprised by the request. "You know my policy. Emergency use only. You've been on these trips before."

Marcus's hands clenched before he forced them to relax. His flash of anger was masked, but Nikki caught it. Whatever business pressures Marcus faced were significant enough to make him push against established rules.

Bear walked a short distance into the meadow, positioning himself on a small rise where the satellite signal would be clearest. His voice drifted back across the open space as he made his report about the wire trap, his tone professional and matter-of-fact as he described the location, the setup, and the potential danger to both horses and riders. Nikki could catch fragments of his conversation: coordinates, descriptions of the activists, and requests for increased patrols.

"He sure loves his animals," Marcus muttered to Nikki. "Sometimes I think he cares more about them than keeping his clients happy."

"One of the activists opposes the use of horses," Nikki replied carefully. "Believes they cause significant environmental damage. I got the impression he wouldn't hesitate to hurt them if he thought it would serve his cause."

"Radical environmentalists," Marcus snorted. "They'd have us all walking everywhere, living in caves. No understanding of practical reality."

Bear returned, carrying the phone. "They'll note the incident in their reports. Send someone out to check the area if there's any further trouble."

"Good," Marcus said, though the tightness in his voice suggested he was hopeful there'd be no need for an official visit "So what's our plan for tonight? Should we do a rotation watch?"

"Maybe it's not necessary." Bear looked at Nikki. "Will Gunner let us know if that pair try another night visit?"

"Absolutely," she said.

Bear gave a relieved smile. "I'm actually glad you brought your dog. He's already proven his worth."

"Yes," Marcus said. "He's good compensation for you being a greenhorn. Even if you're not used to wilderness living, we won't have to worry when we're hunting and you're alone in camp."

Nikki forced a nod. Let Marcus think she was inexperienced. She'd learned to control her emotions, no longer letting frustration bubble out in impulsive words. And being considered powerless could be a good thing. Marcus clearly expected her to stay at camp while the men rode out, but that wasn't going to happen. She had her own agenda.

She ran a hand over Gunner's back, noting how he was staring toward the west. But he wasn't growling so whoever was coming wasn't a foe. Seconds later, the grazing horses also lifted their heads. Two of them even gave welcoming nickers.

Minutes later, Ryan and Doug emerged from the trees. Ryan's horse was moving unevenly, not reaching out with his right hind leg. Years of watching Justin's racehorses had taught her to spot subtle lameness, and Ryan's gray was definitely favoring his leg. But both men looked satisfied, smiling as they stopped beside them.

"Glad you're back," Bear said, his narrowed eyes moving over the horses, checking their condition. "When did Scout lose that hind shoe?"

Ryan swiveled in his saddle, looking confused. "Scout threw a shoe? I didn't notice."

Bear's expression tightened. "Obviously you didn't find it either. And from the way he's walking, you rode him over a lot of rock. Now he's footsore."

Ryan dismounted, his earlier enthusiasm replaced by embarrassment as his cheeks flushed at being called out for poor horsemanship. Nikki felt a pang of sympathy.

Bear moved to Scout's hindquarters and lifted the leg, examining the tender sole with gentle hands. "I've got a couple spare shoes in our cache. What were you doing riding over so much rock?"

Ryan looked at Doug, his mouth opening and closing as if he didn't know what to say.

"You know how Ryan gets when he spots interesting geology," Marcus said, stepping closer to Scout. "He could ride over a rockslide without noticing."

Ryan nodded and started chattering about the rocks here, but unless one had a geology degree, it was tough to follow. He did that a lot, launching into detailed monologues. Nikki had initially thought it was enthusiasm, but perhaps it was his way of deflecting. By boring people with technical details, he could avoid answering uncomfortable questions and hide his lack of wilderness skills. It was easier to sound like a rock expert than admit he could barely stay in the saddle or notice when his horse threw a shoe.

Doug wore an amused smile as he listened to Ryan ramble about metamorphic processes and feldspar crystallization. He and Marcus seemed content to let Ryan do the talking, unlike last night when Ryan had wanted to talk about his father and Marcus had shut him down. In fact, Marcus had already turned away and was headed toward the campfire.

But as Nikki watched his purposeful stride, something odd caught her eye. Doug's new spotting scope lay on top of the stacked firewood. She shifted sideways, pretending to listen to Ryan's explanation of mineral formation, but still able to watch Marcus. When he strode by the wood, he reached out and grabbed the scope, then shoved it into his tent.

Clearly Ryan and Doug had been lying about their activities, and Marcus was helping conceal whatever they'd been doing. There was no mention of photography either, despite Ryan's insistence on bringing his bulky camera case. If they hadn't been looking for deer or taking pictures, what had they done all day? And why was it so secret?

She turned her attention back to the conversation as Bear finished checking Scout's feet and moved to stand by the horse's shoulder. "Spot any big deer?" he asked, his voice gentler now, as if trying to make up for his earlier sharpness.

"No trophy bucks, just some does," Doug said, turning his horse toward the saddle rack. "But we'll glass the ridge again tomorrow."

Nikki watched Gunner's reactions around the two men. He seemed okay with Ryan, but remained aloof with both Doug and Marcus. He was generally an excellent judge of character, and unease prickled along her spine now that she'd caught them in lies about their activities.

It seemed none of Bear's clients could be fully trusted, and she was still uncertain about Bear himself. She needed to talk to Sage alone, find out why the woman was so terrified of the guide, and get the real story about finding Elena's body. Part of her hoped the activists would make another late night visit, giving her a chance to talk to Sage and maybe gain some trust.

Too many questions remained unanswered, too many convenient explanations that didn't quite fit. Whatever these men were hiding, Nikki intended to uncover the truth before someone else ended up dead.

CHAPTER TWELVE

Nikki woke to the soft glow of dawn filtering through the side window of her tent. She lay motionless, listening to Gunner's peaceful breathing, disappointed to realize she'd slept through the entire night. No alerts, no midnight visitors, no chance to talk with Sage.

The sun was already peeking over the horizon, bruising the peaks with red and casting dark shadows across the ridge. Someone was moving outside, the quiet steps drifting across the campsite.

Gunner stretched, showing no signs of having been alarmed during the night. The activists obviously hadn't returned, which meant she'd have to create her own opportunity to reach Sage. The woman held answers about Elena's death, along with the reason she feared Bear.

That fear seemed an important key. If Sage had witnessed Bear doing something to Elena, it could explain her reaction. But if the activist's fear was based on something unrelated, then Nikki was looking at the wrong suspect. Either way, understanding what had frightened Sage so badly was crucial to getting the answers the insurance company needed.

She unzipped her tent and crawled out to find Bear busy with the horses, moving through the routine of morning care. The man never seemed to stop working, his devotion to the animals absolute.

"Morning," she called softly, not wanting to wake the others. "Want some help?"

Bear looked up, his face creasing in a smile. "Always appreciate extra hands. These guys are eager for their breakfast."

They worked together in easy silence, measuring grain into feedbags and checking each horse for any cuts or swellings.

"Scout's still favoring that hind leg," Bear said. "I don't want Ryan riding him today. I'll get a shoe back on him and see how much it helps."

Nikki noticed Bear's tools laid out on a tarp: hammer, rasp, clinchers, nippers, and an assortment of new and used shoes. Clearly he wasn't limited to carrying a simple hoof boot in case a horse threw a shoe. This was a professional setup. "You're also a farrier?" she asked.

"Winter work," Bear said, selecting a shoe then bending down and holding it up to Scout's hoof. "Keeps me busy when the guiding season ends. Most folks around here know I can handle difficult horses, so I stay pretty booked."

His expertise was obvious in the way he handled the tools. It added another layer to her growing respect for him, even as questions about his involvement in Elena's death continued to nag.

The sound of tent zippers announced that others were stirring. Marcus and Doug emerged almost simultaneously, both men looking alert despite the early hour. They gathered around the campfire, speaking in low murmurs while Marcus began brewing coffee.

Nikki returned to her tent and fed Gunner his breakfast, then readied her saddlebags, tossing in everything she might need for a solo ride: phone, bear spray, gun, water, trail bars. She left the saddlebags in her tent and joined the men around the campfire.

Ryan was the last to wake, seeming to have a nose for when breakfast was ready. He crawled from his tent, stretching and offering everyone his characteristic smile. Beautiful morning," he said, breathing deeply of the pine-scented air. "Perfect day for exploring."

Marcus and Doug exchanged glances over their coffee cups then Marcus spoke. "Yes, we're thinking of scouting those ridges to the north. See if we can spot a decent buck."

"Good plan," Bear said. "But Scout needs to stay in camp. He's too tender to ride today, especially over that rocky ground."

"Not a problem," Marcus replied. "Ryan can ride Brownie, and Nikki can stay here and keep an eye on things. Make sure those activists don't try anything."

Nikki bristled at the suggestion. They seemed to want her isolated, left behind while they pursued their own activities. She tamped down her annoyance, forcing her expression to remain neutral, but aware this was a critical moment.

If she let them dictate her movements now, she'd lose the freedom to conduct a thorough investigation. She needed to establish that she couldn't be pushed around or be treated like a liability. Besides, she and Gunner were on watch every night, letting the men sleep. She was already doing her share of security.

"No," she said, her voice firm. "I'm riding out today."

"Why?" Marcus's eyebrow lifted. "You got your insurance photos yesterday. What else do you need?"

Even Bear looked puzzled. "The camp would be safer with someone watching," he said, seeming to think that showing her where Elena had fallen and visiting the ridge should have been sufficient.

"I've been asked to check Elena's water study sites," Nikki said, borrowing Ryan's technique of too much information. "Naturally the university doesn't want her research wasted. They need samples from the original collection points to verify pH levels, test for bacterial contamination, and measure dissolved mineral content."

Marcus, Doug, and even Ryan looked displeased, but as she continued with the technical jargon, their expressions glazed over. The academic barrage was working, making her mission sound both official and tediously boring.

"Elena was specifically studying coliform bacteria levels," Nikki went on, "in relation to seasonal runoff patterns, data crucial for understanding watershed contamination."

Bear gave a slow nod. "Okay, but if you're riding out alone, I need to know your route. Stay on the lower trails, don't climb to any elevation, and be back by mid-afternoon. Weather is changeable and the sun drops fast." His voice carried the authority of someone who'd given this warning before. "And don't cross the stream. If you need any water samples higher up, I'll ride with you tomorrow."

Marcus sighed, seeming to accept that he wasn't getting his own way. But his voice was tight as he gripped his coffee cup. "When will you be back?"

"Mid-afternoon." Nikki said, giving Bear a nod that acknowledged his safety warnings before rising to wash her breakfast dishes. "And it's important work. Elena died for this research. I'm sure none of us want it to be in vain."

No one could object to that without seeming callous about her death, and Nikki looked each of them in the eye before turning to Doug. "I heard that you talked to Elena about water quality the night before she died. Do you remember what she said? It might help locate her study sites, so I can finish up quicker."

"The biologist?" Doug's expression went blank. "I barely remember talking to her, let alone a specific conversation. She wasn't interested in hunting. Rode on her own. Alone in these mountains." He paused, his eyes changing, almost glittering. "Just like you're planning to do."

The way he said it carried an undertone that made Nikki fumble with her dish. The words weren't quite a threat, but close enough. And the implication was clear: Elena had ridden out alone, and look what happened to her.

She straightened her plate against the log, leaving it to air dry. When she glanced up, the men were exchanging more meaningful looks, the type that carried messages she didn't understand but definitely didn't like. Her cover story provided a degree of legitimacy that was hard to challenge but she needed to leave before they thought too hard about the details.

She grabbed her gear and saddled Brownie before anyone could raise more objections. Or ask to see her non-existent water testing kit.

Brownie stood patiently as she tightened the cinch, his honesty a welcome contrast to the tension radiating from the tight circle of men. She could hear their low voices as they discussed the possibility of Ryan riding one of the pack horses, followed by more debate about who would stay to guard camp. Or whether it was even necessary. She buckled on Gunner's orange vest and swung into the saddle, pulling in a relieved breath.

It would be a treat to get away. No more watchful eyes, no more careful conversations, no more pretending to trust men who were obviously hiding secrets. She was free to pursue the truth, starting with Sage Crux.

Once she was hidden by the trees, she changed direction and urged Brownie into an extended trot, heading directly toward the activists' camp. Bear's warnings about staying on lower trails would have to be ignored. Reaching Sage required climbing and crossing terrain he considered off-limits. But answers were waiting in those mountains, and she was determined to find them, no matter what it took.

CHAPTER THIRTEEN

The autumn air carried a bite as Nikki rode Brownie along the same route she and Bear had followed yesterday. A few leaves clung stubbornly to branches, though most had already dropped, carpeting the trail in rustling patches of amber and brown. The granite outcroppings seemed more prominent today, their weathered surfaces catching the slanted sunlight.

Brownie moved confidently beneath her, showing none of the reluctance many horses felt when separated from their herd mates. His ears were pricked with interest rather than nervously swiveling. Some horses would have found reasons to spook or tried to turn back, but Brownie showed both his steady mind and solid training.

She gave his shoulder an approving scratch. Bear had entrusted her with an excellent mount, and she wasn't taking that trust lightly. And Brownie was great with Gunner, who trotted close to the horse's side, his tongue lolling in what looked suspiciously like a grin. He seemed as happy as she was to escape the camp's undercurrents.

When they reached the spot where she and Bear had left the main trail, she reined Brownie onto the game path toward the activists' camp, her initial sense of freedom suddenly replaced with wariness. Had Jake and Sage watched her ride out this morning? Did they know she was alone? And how would the volatile Jake react to a second uninvited visit?

It was impossible to forget the wire trap and the man's hostility toward horses. She scanned for any sign of sabotage that could hurt Brownie, and when a jackrabbit burst from the underbrush, she jumped before recognizing the harmless critter. The thought of Brownie stumbling into a trap, possibly breaking a leg, made her stomach churn. Out here, a broken leg was a death sentence for a horse. There would be no veterinary care, no rescue trailer. Just the terrible choice of leaving him to suffer or putting him down where he lay.

"Easy, just a rabbit," she murmured, though the confident Brownie hadn't even flinched, and it was clear she was speaking more to herself.

The narrow trail wound through stands of pine and fir, filtering the light into shifting patterns. Granite boulders became more frequent, forcing them to pick their way over increasingly rocky terrain.

When she finally reached the clearing where the activists had been camped, she pulled Brownie to a halt. And gaped in shock.

The space was empty. No olive-green tent, no camouflaged tarp, no scattered belongings. Nothing remained to suggest the area had ever been occupied.

She dismounted and trudged around the small clearing, leading Brownie while searching for any trace of campers. Nothing. Not a scrap of wood or even a scraped tree, its bark rubbed by a cache rope. The activists had vanished as if they'd never existed.

"Well, that explains why they didn't visit us last night," she said to Gunner, who was sniffing around a game trail. "They were busy moving camp."

She felt a rising respect for their wilderness skills. Jake and Sage had left no trace of their presence, following the principle that guided responsible outdoor enthusiasts. Despite opposing agendas, they understood and respected the mountains.

But they probably hadn't gone far. Right now, Bear was the only guide in the area, making his camp the target for whatever protest they'd planned. They'd want to stay close while remaining hidden. And they were also on foot.

She clipped Gunner's leash to his collar, encouraging him to work the ground more systematically. He was already interested in one of the game trails and when she said "find" he strained against the leash, keen to follow the scent.

She kept his taut lead in one hand and Brownie's reins in the other, not wanting to release the dog and have to push her horse too fast. Wire traps were a constant concern, and she intended to keep Brownie safe. She was also aware of other horse hazards likely scattered throughout this area: rusted equipment, abandoned shafts, and unstable ground. The activists' sabotage was just one more danger in terrain already riddled with threats.

Gunner led them away from the clearing on what could barely be called a path. The activists had chosen a route that was hostile to horses with steep sides, loose stone, and numerous boulders. They clearly intended to discourage any more visits.

But they hadn't counted on a horse like Brownie. He picked his way over the treacherous footing with the sure-footedness of a goat. Nikki wondered if he carried mustang bloodlines, his intelligence and compact build suggesting wild horse genetics adapted to tough living.

"Good boy," she murmured, giving his neck a pat as he navigated around a jumble of jagged rocks.

Gunner had slowed, seeming to understand her need for caution, moving with confidence but no longer pulling at his leash. After twenty minutes of steady walking, he lifted his head and began testing the air rather than tracking a ground scent. They were getting close.

The terrain around them became increasingly dramatic as they approached the old mining area. Boulders created a maze of twisty passages and alcoves. Vertical rock walls rose on all sides, their surfaces smoothed and weathered by centuries of wind and water.

Rusted pieces of mining equipment lay among the rocks, a testament to the prospectors who'd combed the area for precious metals. The limestone formations and black rock that colored the mountain had been carved by water erosion, creating caves throughout.

Her legs burned with exertion as Gunner led her toward a rock wall, showing no uncertainty despite the dead end. They were only ten feet away when she spotted the opening, a cave entrance nearly hidden by the angle of the rock face and the play of shadows.

She quietly praised Gunner for his work, but her mouth felt dry and she stiffened. The activists had found the ideal spot, with protection from both weather and detection. Good work on their part, as well as her dog's.

But it also meant she was about to confront two people in a confined space. Activists who didn't want to be found. She swallowed, imagining Jake's hostility and the possibility of being trapped in a cave with his waving hatchet.

The smart thing would be to ride away and get help, but Sage was her only lead. Besides, there was no help to be had. She couldn't risk alerting the very men who might be involved in Elena's death. Bear, Marcus, Doug, Ryan—any one of them could be guilty, and she had no way to know which ones she could trust.

Out here in the wilderness, miles from help, she was on her own.

CHAPTER FOURTEEN

Nikki stared at the dark cave, grappling with what to do with Brownie. She couldn't safely lead a horse into an unknown cave with its confining space and uncertain footing. But she couldn't leave him hobbled outside either. There were too many rocky obstacles and they were also close to a steep edge.

She'd have to tie him, which meant finding a sturdy tree. And it would have to be nearby. She didn't want to leave him alone and vulnerable for long.

Motioning for Gunner to follow, she mounted and rode around a scatter of boulders, heading toward a tall pine visible beyond the rocks. The rocks were challenging but Brownie listened to his rider with a trust that was humbling.

The sound of gurgling water grew louder. Minutes later, they spotted a sparkling sheet of water cascading down a rock face, pooling in a natural stone basin. The glittering waterfall created a perfect watering spot for Brownie and Gunner, but something about it made her hesitate. The feeling that she was being watched.

Both Brownie and Gunner were staring at the small waterfall, neither moving to drink, their bodies taut. Then Gunner sat, confirming her fear.

She slowly reached back and unbuckled her left saddlebag, making sure her bear spray was within reach. Any second she expected Jake to burst from hiding, waving his hatchet and ranting about horses destroying the wilderness.

But Gunner's tail wagged, slowly but definitely, and Nikki caught a glimpse of a blond ponytail. Not Jake's dark hair. Relief flooded through her as she realized who was hiding behind that waterfall.

"Hi Sage," she called. "I'm just here to talk."

There was a tense moment of silence. Then Sage edged from behind the sheet of water. She wore a thick fleece jacket over hiking pants, both in earth tones that helped her blend with the rocks. A knit cap covered the top of her head, and sturdy boots gripped the wet stone beside the pool.

She carried a collapsible bucket, obviously intending to collect water from the natural basin before Nikki's arrival had interrupted her routine. Her eyes swept past Nikki, warily scanning the area behind Brownie.

"You're alone?" she asked.

"Yes, just my horse and dog."

"So Bear Hutchins isn't with you?" The relief in Sage's voice was palpable when Nikki shook her head, confirming the woman's terror of the guide

"Where's Jake?" Nikki asked.

"In the cave, still sleeping. But he's within earshot," she added quickly. "If I have to call him."

Nikki understood the warning and knew she didn't have much time to gain Sage's trust. "I need to tell you something." She lowered her voice to a confidential tone. "Yesterday I was introduced as an insurance investigator, but that's not the whole truth. I was hired because Elena Vasquez's husband feels there's something suspicious about her death. I'm not affiliated with Bear or any of the hunters. I'm just here to find out what really happened."

Sage tilted her head, as if weighing Nikki's sincerity. The sound of the waterfall filled the silence while Gunner sat patiently, his calm presence seeming to vouch for peaceful intentions.

"Your dog seems friendly," Sage said. She took a step forward and held out her hand. Gunner immediately trotted up to her, tail wagging. Sage set down her bucket and scratched behind his ears, her voice softening.

"I'd love to have a dog up here," she said. "But Derek Stone sets the rules. Says they're too unpredictable. They bark and scare wildlife, and need too much food and water. He's also worried they'd kill ground-nesting birds."

"There's pros and cons," Nikki said, watching Sage's defenses drop as she continued patting Gunner. "Dogs are good company. And they can be trained."

"Derek thinks of everything in terms of mission effectiveness," Sage replied, then seemed to catch herself. Straightening, she pulled back a step. But when Gunner nudged her hand with his nose, she crouched back down again. "We do try to be invisible observers."

Nikki sensed the loneliness in the young woman, isolated in these mountains with only Jake and their leader's rigid rules. "Well, you're doing a good job of staying invisible," she said, dismounting to put herself on Sage's level rather than looming above. Conversations worked better when both people stood on equal ground. "And you left your last campsite in perfect shape," Nikki added.

Sage smiled at the compliment. "We had to work fast. Jake was freaked out that you found our site. But we were both happy to relocate to the cave system." Her smile slipped. "You won't tell anyone where we are?"

"Absolutely not."

Sage seemed to make her final decision about trust. "It's really comfortable in there," she said, gesturing over her shoulder. "There are multiple entrances. This one by the waterfall is my favorite but our sleeping area is closer to the cliff."

Nikki made an agreeable sound, remembering the hidden entrance that Gunner had found earlier. It seemed that Sage was finally relaxed enough to field some questions. "Can you tell me more about Elena? I understand it's tough to talk about, but it is important."

Sage's nod showed both sadness and frustration. "I really liked that woman. Ran into her a few times. She understood our concerns about what was happening. Wasn't dismissive like most people."

She kicked at a loose stone, sending it clattering. "She told me her findings might stop hunting parties from coming here. Was really excited. But now we'll never know."

"Did she mention anything specific? Her grant covered biodiversity and climate change. Did her findings involve plants or animals? Maybe water?"

"She never said. Wouldn't even tell her husband. But she was excited about it, said she was planning to have a celebratory drink at camp that night." Sage's voice grew pensive. "She seemed happy about what she'd discovered."

Nikki coiled Brownie's reins. Whatever Elena had found was significant enough that she wanted to tell the university before sharing it with anyone else. Professional. But it might also have been dangerous enough to get her killed. And Sage's eyes kept darting around, as if watching for another rider. One that she considered dangerous.

Nikki's voice lifted with urgency. Time was running short. Every extra minute increased the risk that Bear would come looking for her. She needed to know what Sage had seen, what had terrified her so badly, before this opportunity slipped away.

"Look, I need to get back soon. Why are you so afraid of Bear? What did you see?"

Sage crossed her arms, her mouth tightening. Up close, Nikki could see the toll the activists' vigil was taking: prominent cheekbones in a fragile face, dark circles under her eyes, and hollow cheeks that showed she wasn't eating enough. The oversized fleece jacket only emphasized her thinness.

"I never talked to Elena again," Sage said, her voice cracking. I knew she was checking her trail cams. But I saw two horses below the ridge. When one horse stayed in the same spot for hours, I was curious and went to investigate. The horse was fine. Then I walked a little further and..." Her voice dropped to an agonized whisper. "Elena was lying at the bottom, her body all twisted. Smashed. There was so much blood."

Nikki waited, letting Sage gather herself. "What happened to the second horse?" she finally asked.

"Gone. Whoever was riding it had left. I had to hike up to the ridge to call for help. Jake and I used that spot before. It's one of the few places with cell service."

"Did you tell the police about the other horse? What color was it?"

"The same color as the horse Bear was riding yesterday." Sage gave a bitter snort. "They said I could have been mistaken because of the distance. That deer and elk can look like horses. But I know I saw two orange halters."

"And you're sure of the horse's color? A buckskin? Golden? Black mane and tail?"

"Yes, it was the exact same as Bear's horse. Don't you see! Elena's research was going to destroy his business. He had the most to lose if her findings were published. So he made sure they never would."

Sage shook her head and scooped up the bucket. "I think he pushed her off that ridge. And now he knows our campsite overlooked the valley. I'm afraid he might come after me since I told authorities about the second horse. That's why I bugged Jake to move."

Nikki squeezed her eyes shut in dismay. She and Gunner had led Bear to the activists' camp, revealed their vantage point, shown him that someone could have been watching. Maybe he had noticed Sage's fear. Bear was smart enough to know the reason why. And now she might have put Sage in danger.

Still, it was hard to accept. Bear with his gentle hands, his genuine concern for everyone's welfare. Could he really be a killer? Yet if Elena's death hadn't been accidental, the evidence was pointing in an increasingly troubling direction. The possibility that someone had caused her fall couldn't be ignored, even though Nikki hoped she was wrong about her suspicions.

She wet her throat, working out the tightness. Bear expected her back by mid-afternoon, and when she didn't return on schedule, he'd come looking. The thought of him tracking her to this hidden cave, finding Sage again, sent ice through her veins. She had to get back before he decided to search for her.

But first, she needed to make sure Sage understood what was at stake. If someone had killed Elena to protect a secret, they might be willing to silence a witness. Out here, accidents happened: a fall from a cliff, a misstep on loose rock, a sudden disappearance.

The isolation that made these mountains beautiful also made them deadly for anyone who knew too much.

CHAPTER FIFTEEN

"I have to get back to camp," Nikki said. "And you need to stay away." She pictured Doug's spotting scope and Marcus's clenched fists when he'd questioned her about the activists' location. How Marcus had talked about chasing away the activists instead of reporting the wire trap.

"Bear has a rifle and he's probably a crack shot," she added. "And a few of his clients are resentful. They're hunters, Sage." Her hands felt sticky around Brownie's reins as the full implications hit.

An accident could be staged, especially if Sage and Jake attempted another nighttime raid. The campers could claim they thought their nighttime visitor was a ransacking bear—a tragic case of mistaken identity. Few would question experienced hunters claiming they were protecting their horses. And considering how easily local law enforcement had ruled Elena's death an accident, their support for the hunting industry was evident.

"How much longer are you planning to stay?" Nikki asked, hoping Sage would say she was leaving soon. Once off this mountain, the woman would be safe. She could contact the authorities and tell her story to people who could protect her.

"Until the end of the hunting season," Sage replied. "Unless Derek Stone tells us to move on. But Jake already made a trip back for supplies. Brought enough for three more weeks."

Nikki's hopes sank. She couldn't imagine surviving on this barren mountain for that long, especially knowing someone might be hunting for her. And the sheer tedium made her ache. Crouched behind rocks, muscles cramping from holding the same position, fighting the urge to shift when mosquitoes swarmed. The worst part would be the constant vigilance, wondering if every approaching figure could be Elena's killer.

"It's doubtful Bear and his clients will give you anything to film," Nikki said. "They're selective hunters who won't shoot a deer unless it's legal. These aren't poachers desperate for meat or thrill-seekers breaking laws for sport. You could spend weeks out here, finding nothing to help your cause."

"Derek has a long-term plan. And Jake and I intend to do our part." Sage's voice strengthened with righteous conviction, the kind that made rational arguments bounce off like rubber bullets. "Those hunters think they own these mountains, that they can waltz in and slaughter innocent animals. Someone has to protect our wilderness. Or even more will come."

Nikki hid her dismay. Their presence wasn't about logic. It was about ideology, about proving something to Derek Stone and the other activists who hung on their leader's every word. Sage's fear of Bear was secondary to her commitment to the Coalition.

"We're definitely not leaving," Sage added, crossing her arms with the determination of someone who'd made up her mind.

There was no point in arguing. Sage was committed to the cause. Nothing would shake her resolve, regardless of the personal danger.

"What are you eating?" Nikki asked, shifting to practical concerns. Jake may have made a supply run but he couldn't have carried much.

"Dried fruit, trail mix, granola." Sage rubbed at her hollow cheek. "But we supplement with trout. Jake found a beautiful spot where the stream is loaded with fish."

Her expression turned defensive, as if anticipating criticism. "Fish have a lower carbon footprint than land animals. They emit less CO2, and we use traditional hook and line methods, not nets or anything that will damage the ecosystem."

Even in survival mode, they considered their environmental impact. Nikki felt a reluctant respect, even as she worried about Sage's weight loss. At least they'd be safe as long as they remained hidden. Bear and his clients would have no reason to venture so far from the valley where deer grazed.

"Have you seen any of Elena's trail cameras? Or know where she might have placed them?"

"No, we try to stay away from research areas." Sage's shoulders relaxed, her defensiveness melting now that the conversation had shifted from the activists' plans. "We respected what Elena was doing. That's the kind of science we can get behind. We never spotted any of her cameras."

Another dead end. The trail cams had vanished along with Elena's research notes. But Nikki knew she had no time left to stay and talk. She reached into her saddlebag and pulled out three protein bars. "Here, take these."

Sage's eyes sparkled with anticipation then she shook her head. "Jake wouldn't want me eating that. The environmental impact of chocolate production. The packaging waste."

"Maybe you could eat them when he isn't around," Nikki said.

Sage gave an impish smile that showed she wasn't completely locked under Jake's spell. "Maybe I could do that," she said. "I'll hide them in my sleeping bag."

"I need to get back," Nikki said, swinging into the saddle. "Before Bear comes looking for me. He's probably very good at following a trail."

"There's a faster way down," Sage said. "Jake found it when he was exploring some old mining caves. I'll show you."

"But is it okay for Brownie?" Nikki patted her horse's neck, deliberately using the horse's name. If Sage thought of him as a cherished animal rather than another piece of hunting equipment, she might think twice about setting more wire traps. "You guys are amazing climbers," Nikki went on, "but horses have limitations. They have big hearts though and go where the rider tells them. Even if it's dangerous."

"This back trail is rocky but okay," Sage said, her smile including Brownie. "And I won't let Jake set any more tripwires. He didn't want to do that, but Derek insisted." Her shoulders lifted in an apologetic shrug. "We might cut trees though. Block some trails. I can't promise more than that. Derek would have our heads if we didn't do something."

"Please don't try to set our horses free," Nikki said. "And it's not just because of the horses, though they could get hurt wandering. But getting close to Bear and the hunters is too dangerous."

Sage's smile faded as Nikki's warning seemed to sink in—that approaching Bear's camp could get her killed, accident or otherwise. She nodded and pointed toward a gap between two towering slabs. "That way leads back to the main trail. It's way shorter than the route you took to get here."

She led Nikki through a web of boulders and weathered rock where rusted machinery, tailings piles, and prospect holes still scarred the landscape.

"Keep heading down," Sage said, gesturing toward a narrow trail. "I enjoyed your visit," she added, dropping a pat on Gunner's head. "But it's safer for everyone if you don't come back."

Nikki gave a wry nod. What she'd learned about the presence of the second horse changed everything. If Bear had been on that ridge when Elena died, then Sage was at risk from much more than fallout from any sabotage. And the last thing Nikki wanted was to lead the guide to the activists' new camp.

She kept light contact on Brownie's reins, helping him stay collected as he headed downward. The rocks challenged even his sure-footedness, but he picked his way down with his usual agility. Soon the valley was visible below, familiar landmarks reassuring her that camp was less than two miles away.

But she couldn't relax. A blue jay gave its harsh cry, the sound sharp with warning. Chipmunks chattered as she passed, and a squirrel scolded from his perch. Even the wildlife seemed to sense her turmoil.

She checked both sides of the trail, her gaze sweeping between rocky outcroppings and the underbrush. Finally she stopped Brownie and motioned for Gunner to go ahead, irritated that she couldn't control her nervousness and not wanting it to transmit to her horse.

The sun's slanting beams cut through the branches, creating angles of shadow and light. Something glinted on the trail: the distinctive curved shape of a horseshoe. She stared down in surprise. A horseshoe on this remote miner's trail made no sense.

She dismounted and picked up the shoe, turning it over in her hand. No rust on the metal meant it hadn't been lying here long.

Her stomach dropped. It must be Scout's missing shoe. But Marcus had claimed Ryan and Doug were scouting game on the opposite side of the valley, in the grassy, forested areas. This rocky slope was completely wrong for deer. So another lie exposed. Whatever Ryan and Doug had been doing yesterday, it hadn't involved the valley. Or spotting game.

She tucked the shoe into her saddlebag and remounted Brownie, her thoughts whirling. Bear as a possible killer, the undercurrents with his clients, and now more evidence that the three men were lying about their activities. Her PI instincts kicked into high gear. Too many suspects, too many secrets.

The hardest part would be looking Bear in the eye and pretending she still trusted him.

CHAPTER SIXTEEN

An excited whinny drifted across the meadow when Nikki rode into camp. All five horses lifted their heads from the grass, watching Brownie return. He nickered a greeting, and two horses immediately called back, celebrating his return with a welcoming committee's enthusiasm.

Bear strode out to meet her, the wide brim of his cowboy hat shading his expression. "Glad you're back. It's getting late. How many spots did you check?" His gaze swept over Brownie and he gave an approving nod. "Brownie looks good," he added, and his open affection for the horse left an uncomfortable knot in her chest.

"Sampled the river in the valley," she said, the lie coming harder than expected. "And six other sources coming off the cliff." If Bear ventured to the cliff area and found her tracks, those details would give her story credibility.

Steps rustled in the grass. "Welcome back," a smiling Marcus called. "See any sign of the activists?"

"No. Not any deer either." Nikki shifted in the saddle, meeting his gaze. "How did you make out?"

"Stayed here and protected the camp. Again." Marcus's expression soured. "It should be your turn tomorrow. We paid good money to be hunting deer. Not activists."

He said it so casually, as if he really would shoot. And his words were even more chilling now that she saw though his polite manners.

"No problem. I'll watch the camp," she said, dismounting and loosening Brownie's cinch. "But I need to call the insurance office. See what range of water samples the university wants. How many more samples they want me to collect."

"No one uses the phone unless it's an emergency," Marcus said, his words sharp with the expectation of being obeyed.

"I make the rules around here," Bear said. "And it *is* an emergency. To me. I need that insurance company on my side." His eyes locked with Marcus's, the kind of stare-down that settled dominance. Marcus looked away first.

Nikki's hands stilled over the cinch, surprised by Bear's response. He was supporting her, which meant he wasn't suspicious of her activities. The realization brought a measure of calm, along with relief that she'd be able to update Justin.

She led Brownie to the saddle rack, feeling the tension ease from her shoulders. She'd made it back to camp without raising any suspicion about where she'd been. When she pulled off the saddle, dried sweat marked his back but his chest was cool to her touch. She quickly brushed away the marks and began cleaning his feet, understanding his eagerness to join his friends. Brownie had carried her safely all day, and he deserved this time to graze. It was best for horses to eat little and often to keep their digestive system healthy, and after the long ride he needed grass.

Only fifteen feet away, Bear and Marcus continued bickering. Marcus still sounded annoyed that Nikki was allowed to use the phone and not him, and she wondered if Bear would relent.

Keeping his clients happy was important, and Marcus was the decision maker. If he decreed that they weren't coming back, Doug and Ryan would listen.

She had to wonder why they kept returning at all. For men who complained about everything from the food to the activists to the lack of trophy bucks, they showed remarkable loyalty to this particular guide. Most dissatisfied clients would have found a new outfitter years ago.

Bear strode over, removed his hat and wiped his brow. "Thanks for taking care of Brownie. Nice to see he has all his shoes. He and Scout have a smaller foot than the others, and I only have one spare left in their size."

Nikki's gaze flickered to her saddlebags, the idea crystallizing. Tonight, when the camp slept, she'd sneak back and check if the shoe she'd found matched Scout's foot. If it did, she'd know for certain that Ryan and Doug had been riding on that miners' trail. And nowhere near the valley where they'd claimed to be scouting.

She didn't know what it would prove, but in her experience, people usually had a reason to lie. The more elaborate the deception, the bigger the secret. And men willing to coordinate alibis might be capable of far worse than dishonesty.

Bear replaced his cowboy hat and turned away, pausing to call over his shoulder. "Supper's going to be baked beans and toasted cheese buns. And of course Marcus and Doug will be passing around their whisky. An evening ritual for them."

The word 'ritual' made Nikki straighten, her hand gripping the hoof pick. Sage had mentioned that Elena planned to have a celebratory drink the night before she died. Had liquor loosened her tongue? And had Bear been listening when she revealed her discovery? It wouldn't be the first time someone spilled secrets after a few drinks.

She grabbed Brownie's hobbles, so deep in thought she didn't notice that Bear had returned with his satellite phone. He waited until she hobbled Brownie in the meadow then led her to a spot a hundred feet from the horses.

"There's usually good reception here," he said, extending the phone's antenna. "As long as the wind isn't too bad. Wait for the signal acquisition—this light here—then dial like normal, but you need the country code first." He demonstrated the sequence, his calloused fingers moving over the keypad with surprising dexterity. "Battery indicator's here. If it gets low, there's a backup in my tent."

He handed her the phone and walked back toward camp, not hovering as she'd feared. The privacy was a gift she'd hoped for, but hadn't expected.

She punched in Justin's number, her fingers drumming against the phone's case, hoping he'd answer. Meadow grass swayed in the breeze, and she found herself plucking at the long strands, then blowing at the seed heads.

Justin picked up on the fifth ring, emergency vehicles wailing in the background. "Hey, can't talk long," he said, his voice taut. "Everything okay?"

"Gunner and I are fine," she said. "But I met the person who found Elena's body. She says there were two riders at the cliff that day, but only Elena's horse remained."

A long pause was filled with distant radio chatter, and Justin asking someone to hold up. Then his voice strengthened. "Two riders?"

"The second horse was gone when help arrived," Nikki added. "But someone else was there when Elena died." She kept her voice low, glancing toward camp where it looked like supper was almost ready. "Can you check with the local authorities? Find out who was first on scene, whether someone took Elena's research notes and cameras? And who retrieved Elena's horse?"

"You suspect someone at your camp?"

"Yes." Nikki's throat tightened. "The guide. But he doesn't know I'm checking any of this."

"Jesus, Nik. You need to—"

Static crackled through the connection, the sirens screaming louder. "I have to go," Justin said. "But I'll make those calls. Be careful. Don't take unnecessary risks."

The line went silent, leaving Nikki alone in the meadow with the satellite phone and her growing suspicions. She retracted the antenna and trudged back toward camp, to the smell of wood smoke and beans and burnt buns.

Tonight she'd sit by that fire, smile and drink and see what truths emerged when alcohol lowered the men's guard. The prospect left her dragging her feet, but Elena Vasquez deserved justice.

CHAPTER SEVENTEEN

The campfire hissed and crackled, casting shadows across the men's faces. Wind moaned through the pine branches, and somewhere an owl called while the horses shifted restlessly on the picket line.

Nikki leaned against the rough log, watching how the shadows seemed to move just beyond the firelight's reach. The horses' fidgeting had nothing to do with activists. She knew Sage and Jake were safely hidden miles away in their cave. Whatever was making the animals uneasy came from something else, something that made the darkness feel alive.

"Top up your cup, Nikki?" Marcus asked, the whisky bottle catching the light as he raised it in the air.

"Sure, thanks." She held out her cup, hiding the fact that she'd been nursing the same drink for an hour. Gunner lay at her feet, and there was a convenient spot between her boot and his shoulder where she could dump the liquor.

"We'll have to slow down soon or there's a chance our stash will run out," Marcus said, though his crooked grin suggested he wasn't serious.

His friends chuckled, clearly having no intention of stopping their drinking. Nikki forced a smile, trying to appear relaxed and sociable. Only Bear looked removed, barely touching his whisky and showing no desire to join the festivities. Ever alert, his gaze kept shooting to the horses.

She cradled her cup, resigned to the fact that she couldn't risk probing about a second horse at the bottom of the ridge. Bear was too observant. One wrong word and he'd see through her questions. And he would be a formidable adversary with his knowledge of these mountains and his skill with firearms.

Ironically, his restraint might be because of her presence. As the insurance investigator, her report would affect potential coverage. The very cover story that gave her access to the camp might also be keeping her primary suspect sober.

But Bear's concern over the horses left her with a twinge of guilt. The man simply couldn't relax.

"Don't worry," she said, trying to sound casual. "I doubt the activists will return after Gunner scared them off."

"I hope they come back." Marcus jabbed at the fire with a pointed stick, almost falling as he leaned forward. Sparks exploded in bursts, scattering embers that reflected in his eyes like needle points of malice. "We'd finally have something to shoot! And we wouldn't have to field dress. No gutting, no skinning, no cleaning up the mess."

"Yeah, just drop their bodies in a cave somewhere," Doug added, his voice slurred. "Let the scavengers have them. And good riddance."

Nikki pressed the cup to her lips, hiding her discomfort. The men's discussion of murder was disgusting, but their darkening humor meant the liquor was doing its work. Their inhibitions had dissolved, revealing the potential for violence that lurked beneath their manners. She needed to take advantage, even as her instincts screamed to retreat to her tent.

"Are there caves close by?" she asked, feigning innocence.

"Yeah, the mountains are riddled with them," Doug said, taking another swig. He was talking much more than usual, his words loosened by alcohol. "Deep shafts that drop hundreds of feet. Some have passages that go for miles. Mazes where people get lost and die. Perfect places for bodies to disappear."

His snicker was a little too long, like someone savoring a private joke. "Local rescue teams rarely attempt cave recoveries," he said. "Too dangerous. So stay away. I've never been up there and don't intend to go. Leave that kind of terrain to the dead researchers."

Doug's callous reference to Elena made Nikki's teeth grit. He spoke of the woman's death like it was nothing more than an inconvenience. She filed away his cliff denial, knowing that once she checked the horseshoe, she'd know if he was lying. But his words sounded more like a warning than drunken chatter.

She pulled out some marshmallows and spread them on the grill, carefully turning them until they turned a golden brown. Around her, the men traded ribald jokes punctuated by loud guffaws, including several crude comments about what their wives didn't need to know. Marcus laughed the loudest, his eyes sliding toward Nikki with a speculative gleam that made her skin crawl.

The atmosphere had shifted. Now, it was her versus them. And they all knew it.

"You can hold your liquor better than most women," Doug said, accepting a marshmallow. "Most get tipsy after a couple drinks."

"Speaking from experience?" Nikki asked, keeping her voice light.

"Elena had a few drinks one night and was pretty wasted." Doug's contemptuous laugh held no warmth. "Lightweight."

Bear rose to his feet, apparently having had enough of the increasingly dark conversation. "I'm going to check the horses and turn in," he said. "Make sure that fire's out when you're done. And don't drink any more if you plan on hunting tomorrow."

Nikki watched him leave, disappointed that there'd been no chance to ask him any questions. But then, he'd barely had any liquor.

Ryan had also been drinking less than the others, though he looked happy, flashing a goofy smile as he stuffed marshmallows into his mouth. He was stoned, she realized, likely on edibles, so easy to carry on horseback. She shifted closer to him, settling into the space Bear had vacated. The rough log was still warm from Bear's back, and she couldn't help questioning if he was her ally or her biggest threat. Around this fire, she was never sure who to trust.

"Did you have a good day checking out formations?" she asked.

Ryan's smile turned dreamy. "Yeah...my father would be so proud. Keeping the claim alive."

Nikki leaned forward, lowering her voice as she pretended to pat Gunner. "What sort of claim?"

"Hey, Ryan!" Marcus's voice cut like glass. "Time for bed. You know how hard it is for you to get up in the morning."

Ryan blinked. "Yeah, okay." He struggled to his feet, almost falling on the hot grill as he gathered a handful of marshmallows before wobbling toward his tent.

"You've been asking a lot of questions for an insurance agent," Doug said, pinning her to the log with his stare. "Better be careful. These mountains can be dangerous for people who get curious about things that are none of their business."

Nikki forced herself to hold his stare, though her heart thudded against her ribs. "The insurance company is paying me to ask questions," she said "I'm just trying to be thorough."

Doug rose, unfolding with the fluid grace of someone sober despite the evening whisky. His smile was razor-thin. "Yeah, just make sure you don't get too thorough."

Marcus also rose, much more unsteady on his feet, but just as keen to leave. Neither of them bothered with the basic courtesy of saying good night, leaving her alone with the dying fire and a ball of fear stuck in her throat.

She'd crossed a line tonight, and there was no taking it back. Marcus and Doug weren't just drunk hunters talking tough. They were dangerous men who seemed prepared to make good on their threats.

And help was days away.

CHAPTER EIGHTEEN

Nikki lay unmoving, staring up at the tent's ceiling. Moonlight filtered through the nylon, casting shadows that shifted with every gust of wind. Sleep felt impossible with her body jumpy and her mind racing. The men's casual discussion of murder, Doug's lies about the cliffs, Ryan's slip about the mining claim. All pieces she didn't understand.

Gunner twitched in his sleep and snoring drifted from one of the tents. Probably Marcus sleeping off his liquor. A rodent rustled through the grass alongside her tent, and the mosquito that had been circling her head finally found her ear, its high-pitched whine adding to her sleeplessness.

Her muscles ached from the long day in the saddle. But physical discomfort was nothing compared to her unease. The more she was around these men, the more they left her wary. They talked about murder like it was sport, and the four remaining days until she could ride back to the trailhead felt agonizingly distant.

The horseshoe lay beside her sleeping bag. If it matched Scout's hoof, it would prove that Doug and Ryan were lying. She didn't know if or how that remote mining trail was connected to Elena's death, but people didn't conceal their whereabouts without reason. And she couldn't lie here any longer without knowing the truth.

She reached for her jacket, the sleeping bag rustling with the movement. The sound seemed loud and she stilled, listening for any sign that she'd disturbed the men. After waiting a long cautious minute, she pulled the jacket over her T-shirt and drew in a fortifying breath. The thought of leaving the security of her tent made her heart pound, but she needed the cover of darkness.

She raised the tent zipper, inch by inch, wincing at each metallic rasp. Cool air hit her face as she peered out, checking the camp. All the other tent flaps were closed, their occupants hopefully sleeping off the alcohol.

Gunner rose, instantly alert and tail wagging. He loved midnight adventures, and she was appreciative of his company. "Heel," she whispered.

They slipped through the tent door and headed toward the picket line. The ground was cold beneath her bare feet, and she winced when rocks bit into her soles. A crescent moon provided enough light to see the horses while stars blazed brilliant in the mountain air.

Brownie lifted his head and nickered, hopeful for more grain. She froze at the telltale sound and glanced over her shoulder at the row of tents. Bear would be the first to investigate. But his door remained zippered.

She approached Scout slowly, trying not to rush, even though every instinct screamed to get back to her tent. But she didn't know this horse well and she spent some time scratching his neck before sliding her hand along his back and down his hind leg.

He obligingly lifted his foot, well trained like all of Bear's horses. She fumbled with the shoe, her cold hands shaking from nerves as much as the night chill. Her fingers were clumsy as she positioned the metal against his hoof, nearly dropping the shoe before managing to hold it steady.

Her heart sank at the unmistakable match. It was a perfect fit.

She released Scout's hind foot and moved back to his head, giving him an absent pat. So now she knew Doug and Ryan had been on that old miners' trail, nowhere near where they claimed to be scouting deer. What that meant, she had no idea.

A sharp smack cut the night, followed by Gunner's yelp. Movement rippled along the picket line as Scout pinned his ears and lashed out again, this time connecting with thin air.

"Oh hell," she breathed, hurrying to her dog. She'd told Gunner to heel and he'd been doing exactly that, proof that stress had dulled her judgment. Between the sleepless night, the adrenaline, and her focus on the evidence, she'd lost track of the basics—like keeping her partner away from a horse known to kick.

"Sorry, buddy," she whispered, running her hands over Gunner's ribs. He seemed fine, almost embarrassed by the incident and gave her hand a lick, as if apologizing for his yelp. Then he wagged his tail and danced around, moving normally but keeping a wary distance from Scout.

"Did you hear something? Was it the activists?"

Bear's deep voice made her jerk upright. She hadn't heard him approach and she slipped the shoe into her jacket pocket before wheeling to face him.

"No," she said. "Thought I heard something but it was a false alarm. I was just checking the horses when Scout kicked Gunner."

"Don't blame Scout," Bear said, his gaze swinging to Gunner.

"I'm not."

"Poor horse has been defensive ever since coyotes tried to hamstring him," Bear bent over Gunner, running gentle hands over his body. "Your dog seems okay though. Strange that he's avoided Scout until now. He seemed to have a good read on all the horses."

"My fault. I told him to heel," Nikki admitted, her feelings jumbled by Bear's concern. It was hard to accept that a man who cared so much for animals could be a killer. But Justin's warning echoed in her mind: Dangerous people were often the ones who appeared the most trustworthy.

Another tent zipper rose. Moments later, Marcus rushed up, with gleaming eyes and a swinging rifle. The smell of whisky hung over him like a cloud.

"Which way?" Marcus asked, turning his rifle toward the trees. "Let me take a shot."

Bear reached out and pried the rifle from the man's hands. "There's no one here," he said. "And I'll keep that rifle until morning."

Marcus glowered, the tension between the two men crackling. Nikki guessed a showdown was coming, a test of wills that would show who really controlled this camp. Marcus's hands clenched into fists, but he didn't grab for his gun.

Instead, his gaze dropped to her bare legs where her jacket ended mid-thigh. His smile turned slow and predatory, nothing civilized about it despite his expensive dental work.

"Nice legs," he said, his voice thick with alcohol and intent. "Let's go back to my tent. I've got more whisky and we can keep each other warm."

"No thanks," Nikki said, though her pulse hammered and Gunner's low growl confirmed what her instincts already knew. Marcus was drunk, unpredictable, and viewed her as easy prey.

Bear immediately stepped to her side, the rifle cradled in his arms. The irony wasn't lost on her—finding safety with the very man who might have killed Elena.

Marcus's smile turned to a glower as he looked between her and Bear. He clearly wasn't getting what he wanted. "Frigid bitch," he muttered as he turned away, the words loud enough to be heard. His voice carried the frustration of a man used to getting what he wanted, when he wanted it.

"I'll talk to him in the morning," Bear said quietly. "When he's sober."

Nikki gave a grateful nod. Whatever else Bear might be, he was the only person standing between her and Marcus's drunken aggression. Ryan was too passive and she didn't know what Doug would do. Whether he'd intervene or simply watch. Or worse, join in.

She hoped she'd never have to find out.

CHAPTER NINETEEN

Nikki balanced the coffee pot in one hand and a bucket in the other, and headed toward the stream, glad to have the simple task of gathering water for the breakfast dishes. Frost still clung to the grass and the morning air was crisp and clean, a welcome relief after last night's ugliness.

Gunner's growl made her stop short. She turned to see that Marcus was following, his smile firmly in place.

"Bear insists I owe you an apology," he said, hands spread in a gesture of contrition. "I admit I drank too much. And you're a beautiful woman."

Nikki arched an eyebrow, determined not to make it easy.

"So, sorry if I offended you," Marcus said. "Or if you misunderstood anything that happened. But this was meant to be a guy's trip, a time to cut loose." His words suggested the fault lay with her interpretation and her very presence, and she felt herself bristling.

"Of course," she said, her voice saccharine sweet. "Boys will be boys."

Marcus's smile slipped as if he knew she was mocking him. However, he pressed on. "I understand you're staying back today to watch camp while we scout game. Thank you. I appreciate that."

Nikki gave a gracious nod. But the arrangement suited her. She wanted to call Justin and hear the official report about Elena's death. And frankly she was looking forward to having time alone.

They walked back to camp, Marcus insisting on carrying the bucket of water in what appeared to be a gentlemanly gesture. They maintained their politeness while Gunner remained openly wary. Marcus filled her with revulsion, and her dog's unhappiness with his presence only confirmed her feelings.

Bear gave Marcus an approving nod, clearly believing everything had been smoothed over. Meanwhile, Ryan bounced around camp with his typical cheerfulness, eager to ride out and take pictures of more rocks.

"Hey," he whispered, pulling Nikki aside while the others saddled their horses. "I've got a stash of magic mushrooms in my tent if you get bored. Help yourself."

Nikki gave him a sincere thanks. His offer gave her a good excuse to search his tent. The mushrooms also explained his euphoric moods and why he was the only one without a rifle. Either he chose not to carry one while under the influence, or Bear had made that decision for him.

Bear approached, carrying his satellite phone, his lined face showing the fatigue of someone who'd been up early. Circles shadowed his eyes, and Nikki wondered if he'd slept at all. As the guide, he carried all the responsibility. The safety of his clients, the security of his horses, and the tensions that had erupted last night.

"I'm putting this by your tent so you can call the insurance office," he said. "Keep Gunner close. I don't like leaving you alone with those activists around." He stared at her for a moment, as if there was more he wanted to say, but just gave a short nod and turned away.

Fifteen minutes later, the four men rode from camp, sitting tall, with rifles in their scabbards. All except Ryan. When a covey of quail exploded from the grass, Scout sidestepped and Ryan almost slid off. He wasn't much of a rider and it was no wonder his horse had thrown a shoe. Ryan did little to guide or collect his horse, leaving Scout to make his own decisions about potential threats. A horse with a weak, inattentive rider learned quickly that he was on his own.

Nikki breathed a sigh of relief when they disappeared in the trees. The October morning was stunning and now much more enjoyable. Golden leaves caught the slanting sunlight and busy squirrels chattered from the branches. Without the men's unsettling company, she could almost forget why she was here.

She made another pot of coffee and settled on the camp log, savoring the peacefulness. No traffic, no smog, no crawling commute to the office. And no hunters. A glance at her watch showed it was still early, but Justin didn't sleep much. Unlike her limited power as a PI, he could obtain answers quickly. Few people stood up to him, even territorial sheriffs.

First, though, she wanted to hear a feminine voice. Sonja would be finished feeding her animals and Nikki craved normal conversation. She might as well take advantage of having access to the satellite phone, even though Bear might guess it hadn't been an insurance call.

She carried the phone into the meadow, walking past Brownie and the two pack horses to the spot where Bear had said the reception was strongest. The horses lifted their heads then returned to their grazing, sharing her contentment at remaining in camp.

Sonja answered on the second ring, her voice bright with pleasure."Nikki! How's it going? I was just thinking about you."

They chatted for a few minutes about Sonja's latest rescue animals and Nikki's current location, enjoying the relaxing flow of friendship.

"Wait, you're being paid for this?" Sonja laughed. "Horses, mountains and camping. Sounds like your dream trip."

"It's great," Nikki said.

"What's wrong?" Sonja asked, her psychic instincts immediately picking up that something was amiss.

Nikki found herself explaining about Elena's death, how she was certain the researcher had been murdered despite the official ruling. "And I don't trust the men I'm with," she said. "Including the guide."

Sonja was quiet for a moment, and when she spoke her voice was subdued. "And Gunner is no match for a rifle."

That stark truth made Nikki gulp. In the background, she could hear Ginger barking, and she wished that both Sonja and her pit bull were here.

"What was the biologist's name?" Sonja said. "Let me see if I can pick up something." Her psychic abilities had proven remarkably accurate over the years, often providing insights that conventional investigation missed.

"Elena Vasquez," Nikki said.

She listened to the clicking of computer keys as Sonja searched online, looking for photos or biographical information that might help her connect with Elena's energy. Then silence stretched, long enough that Nikki began to think they'd lost the connection.

"She was happy before she died," Sonja finally said, her voice solemn. "Did she have a dog with her?"

"No, but she was riding a horse."

"I'm just seeing squirrels, birds, and a small brown animal. And happiness."

Nikki sighed. Elena might have been happy before her death, but her ending certainly wasn't. And she hadn't brought along a dog. Bear didn't allow them. Or at least that's what he'd said.

Nikki's mind raced through possibilities. Had Elena brought a pet on that spring trip? Maybe her dog had attacked Scout, not coyotes. Bear had mentioned the incident several times, but what if it had really been a dog? That might explain some anger, a desire for revenge. But that theory quickly fell apart. Normal people didn't kill over a dog bite, no matter how much they loved their horse. And Elena's husband hadn't mentioned a pet.

Nikki shook her head, dismissing the crazy theories. She was grasping at straws, trying to find motives. "Anyway," she said, "tell me about that injured donkey you mentioned."

She and Sonja talked for a few more minutes, making plans to meet for lunch once Nikki returned, then ended the call.

Nikki stretched out on the meadow grass, feeling more optimistic after talking to her friend, even though Sonja's psychic reading didn't make sense. The sun-warmed ground felt good against her back, and she savored the sweet scent of late-blooming wildflowers. For a while, she simply let herself enjoy being alive in this place. But the peaceful interlude couldn't last. She still had a job to do. She checked her watch. Time to see what Justin had learned.

Her call went straight to Justin's voicemail. She wandered over to the horses and gave Brownie and the two pack horses some attention. The pack animals were much larger than Brownie, with big feet and the bone structure needed to carry heavy loads. However, they were sweet fellows, happy to lower their heads and have their jaws scratched.

She checked their hobbles. All secure. No signs of chafing. Bear had invested in sheepskin padding to protect their legs, another sign of his thoughtfulness. The man might be a killer, but he truly cared for his animals. And she kept wondering how he'd react if Elena's dog had bitten Scout.

She strode back to the phone and tried Justin again.

This time he answered. "Hey Nik," he said, his voice low and warm in the way that always made her heart skip. "How are things today?"

"Great," she said, feeling a smile lift her mouth.

"Wish I could be up there. What's your horse like?" He understood better than most how much depended on having a trustworthy mount in rough country.

"Brownie's great. And Gunner is having a good time too." Except for when he was kicked by Scout, but she didn't want to get into that. Not with all the questions swirling in her head about Elena possibly having a dog, and what role that might have played in her death.

"Good to hear." Justin's tone changed as he talked to someone in the background. She could hear him giving crisp instructions followed by an office door shutting. The sounds of his city detective world felt far removed from her peaceful meadow.

"I have that information from the local sheriff," he said. "Want me to read you the report?"

"Please."

"Cause of death: fall from height, massive trauma consistent with impact. Helicopter was first on scene after emergency call from witness. Victim pronounced dead on impact. Forestry Service personnel led bay horse, fifteen-one hands, back to guide's camp and advised of the accident. Authorities removed personal belongings from saddlebags and released them to victim's spouse twenty days later."

Justin paused. "Statement from Sage Crux: Discovered body, hiked to cell phone service, called 911. Thought she saw two horses at base of cliff. A bay and a buckskin. Note: area has a healthy population of deer and elk which commonly graze there and are the same color."

Convenient, Nikki thought, noting what wasn't mentioned. "Any reference to research notes or trail cameras? Or a dog?"

"No. Why?"

"The victim was conducting an environmental study. She should have had notebooks, cameras, maybe recording equipment. If that stuff wasn't in her saddlebags, then someone took it before the authorities arrived. Maybe whoever was riding the second horse."

"But the sheriff is correct," Justin said. "A deer could look like a buckskin horse, especially if the witness was upset or viewing from a distance. And did you check with the victim's husband about her belongings? Maybe he has them."

"Of course I checked with him," Nikki said, recognizing the edge in her voice. "That was the first thing I did."

Justin drew a long breath. "Sorry, Nik. I know you're thorough. But you might be looking for something that isn't there."

She rose, pacing a circle in the grass. Justin was siding with the authorities, dismissing what Sage had seen. But then again, there was no proof. And detectives dealt with cold hard facts.

"I guess," she said, her irritation deflating. "I'm just a bit on edge. Afraid the death wasn't an accident. And these men..." She trailed off, not sure how to explain the undercurrents.

"What about them?" Justin's voice sharpened. "Are you safe? Is the guide negligent? I can call in some favors, pressure the sheriff to reopen the case. Should you get out of there?"

"I'm fine," she said. "I don't know anything concrete, just suspicions. But the report was a big help. And I'll keep in touch. If anyone asks, you're my contact at the insurance office and we need to talk about water samples."

Justin chuckled despite his worry. "Got it. I love you, Nik."

"Love you too."

She ended the call, staring across the meadow, feeling more alone than ever. Her churning thoughts wouldn't quiet. It seemed Elena's research might have been valuable enough to kill for, important enough that someone had risked staying at the scene to retrieve it. But what could a researcher have discovered that was worth committing murder?

The horseshoe felt cold against her fingers as she touched it through her jacket pocket. Doug and Ryan had lied about their whereabouts, but that didn't seem connected to Elena's death. The missing trail cams might shed some light if she could only find one.

She just had to be careful not to push her luck. Doug's threat had been delivered with the grim certainty of a man who'd made good on such promises before.

CHAPTER TWENTY

Nikki scanned the horizon one more time, checking for any sign of returning riders. But there was no movement except for grass swaying in the breeze. Reassured she was alone, she jogged to Ryan's tent and tugged up the zipper.

The smell slammed her in the face. Ryan hadn't bothered to open any side vents and the musty air reeked of wet clothes, foot odor, and that distinct guy smell of someone who'd skipped deodorant. A baggie containing magic mushrooms and gummies sat at the end of his sleeping bag. Enough supply to last for weeks. No wonder he bounced in the saddle like a tennis ball.

His saddlebags were with his horse, but his camping gear was spread out: sleeping bag, pad, spare clothes, and a rolled slicker which he'd been using as a pillow. She crawled further into the tent, almost bumping into something tucked in the corner. She recognized his black camera case but now it had a compass and rock hammer placed on top, as well as a well-creased plastic bag, the items positioned like a shrine.

She memorized the bag's position before picking it up. Inside were several black and white photos along with folded notes. The first picture showed a grim man in work clothes standing beside what was clearly a mining claim, tools scattered around a rocky outcrop.

She could make out a pickaxe driven into the ground, coils of rope, and a wooden wheelbarrow filled with ore samples. Near the mouth of a shaft sat what looked like a hand-crank winch. The man's sleeves were rolled up, his hands dark with the kind of dirt that never fully washed away. Behind him, timber supports framed the entrance to what must have been a productive mine. The resemblance to Ryan was unmistakable.

The second photo made her wonder where Ryan got his good humor. Another stern-looking man stared back, his hard eyes completely devoid of fun. On the back, someone had written a message, the ink faded with time: 'Keep it in the family. Don't be the one who loses it.'

She skimmed through a few more notes, not wanting to pry into anything too personal, but the findings were obvious. Ryan's mining bloodlines ran deep, stretching back generations. And from what she glimpsed, his family hadn't let any of them forget it. There were constant reminders about living up to the family name, about not being a weak link.

She replaced everything as she'd found it and slipped from the tent, taking an appreciative breath of fresh air. The pine-scented breeze felt like a blessing after the staleness of the tent, washing away not just the odors but the oppressive weight of Ryan's legacy.

She remembered how emotional he'd become that first night around the campfire before Marcus had shut him down. Now she understood. Trying to make ancestors proud was a heavy burden. Her own family had influenced her career choice, but she'd never felt pressured.

Sometimes she wished her undercover cop father was still alive to see that she'd become a PI, following his investigative footsteps. Or if he'd have been proud that she'd solved his murder. But she didn't carry around pictures and notes and hide geological tools in a fake camera case.

She pushed aside her empathy for Ryan. Whatever his family pressures, she had a job to do. And that included camp chores. She focused on gathering kindling for the evening fire and periodically checking on the three horses. Around noon, she led them to the stream for a drink. It was a little tough to juggle the three lead lines but Gunner helped, enjoying the herding job.

The river curved around smooth rocks, creating small pools where the horses could dunk their muzzles and play with the water. Trees provided dappled shade along the banks, and water bubbled invitingly.

It was an oasis of calm, and the perfect time to take advantage of being alone. After the horses had their fill, she led them back to the meadow. Then she returned to the river and washed her hair, luxuriating in the simple pleasure of feeling clean.

Gunner also plunged in, swimming circles around her and cutting the water with powerful strokes. When he trotted back onto the bank, he rolled and shook, spraying water and acting more like a puppy than a serious working dog. Clearly he also enjoyed this alone time.

The sun slanted from the south, providing welcome warmth, and the breeze helped dry her hair. She lay back on a granite slab, relaxed and almost dozing. Insects buzzed and occasionally a fish jumped. The peaceful sounds lulled her into a rare state of contentment. Until Gunner's low growl snapped her alert.

She sat up, shading her eyes, and spotted two riders approaching camp. Bear's buckskin was instantly recognizable. She hurried out to meet them, noting Ryan's slumped posture in the saddle.

"Ryan took a spill," Bear explained, his voice carrying a hint of irritation. "Sprained his ankle and wanted to come back to camp." The way he said it suggested he had doubts about the severity of Ryan's condition, or whether there was any injury at all.

Ryan slid clumsily from his horse, making a big show of not landing on his right foot. "Sorry to be such a bother," he said, though he didn't look particularly sorry. Relief was written all over his face at being back in the comfort of camp rather than struggling to keep up with the more experienced riders. "Just needed to get back and elevate my leg."

Bear's expression suggested he thought Ryan was being soft, but his professionalism won out. "Nikki, could you unsaddle Scout for him? I need to get back to Doug and Marcus."

She nodded, taking Scout's reins while Bear swung back into his saddle and trotted off.

After tending to Ryan's horse, Nikki carried his saddlebags back to camp. They felt surprisingly light and she positioned them on the ground in front of Ryan. He immediately propped his left foot on the bags, and she hid her smile. He couldn't even remember which ankle was supposed to be injured. Obviously he'd been searching for an excuse to return to camp and had grabbed the ruse of a sprained ankle. No wonder Bear had been skeptical.

Of course, Ryan hadn't brought his geological case on the ride. She'd seen it sitting in his tent. Little wonder he'd grown bored with scouting wildlife when his real interests lay elsewhere. She didn't understand why he'd left the case then realized that Bear had been with the men today. When Ryan rode the mining trail with Doug, he could study rocks without having to maintain the charade of being interested in hunting.

She felt sorry for Ryan, eager to join his friends on these expeditions but having no interest in hunting or horses.

"Water?" she offered, pulling out a bottle, feeling even more protective of him after seeing those family photos. It explained his desire to please, even when Marcus treated him poorly.

"Actually I'd prefer something stronger from the bag in my tent." Ryan gave her a conspiratorial wink. "Especially since Marcus and Bear aren't around to give a lecture. And you look like someone who can keep a secret."

Nikki laughed and headed toward his tent. She wouldn't add to his troubles by judging his coping mechanisms. She retrieved his stash then spread peanut butter on a camp roll, anticipating he'd soon have the munchies.

Ryan became increasingly talkative as the gummies took effect. They chatted about the weather, politics, and the challenges of environmental regulations. He shared stories about his university professors, rare rock formations, and even his struggles with learning to ride, grateful for someone who wasn't constantly criticizing his outdoor skills.

"You know," Ryan said, shifting to prop his ankle more comfortably on the saddlebags, "this is even nicer than the spring trip. Marcus couldn't come then because he was going through his divorce. It was just me and Doug. There was less bossiness, if you know what I mean."

"Marcus seems accustomed to running things," Nikki said. "And he does seem capable. Even Bear listens to him."

"Yeah," Ryan said glumly. "Marcus is good at everything. He was like that in university too. I introduced him to my dad once, and of course Marcus found a piece of quartz with gold flecks in it. He picked it up like it was nothing. Dad was more impressed with him in ten minutes than he'd been with me in years." He gave a rueful sigh. "Now Marcus comes up here and acts like he's some kind of mountain man, talking hunting strategy and reading the terrain with Bear. While I can barely find my own horse unless it's a different color."

Nikki grabbed the chance to turn the conversation to Elena. "It's always easier to recognize a gray horse. Or a buckskin," she added, watching his expression. "Do you usually ride Scout on your trips?"

"I just ride whatever horse Bear brings me." He rubbed his forehead trying to remember. "I think they've always been brown, not gray. All I know is that Scout's trot is bumpier than some of the others I had."

Nikki hid her disappointment. So far, the only rider of a buckskin horse was Bear. But she wasn't giving up. Ryan was finally talking freely, and she needed to pull out every bit of information while she had this chance.

"It must be nice up here in the spring. Did you talk to Elena much during that trip?"

"Not really. She wasn't interested in geology. Went to bed early. Only had drinks with us once, and she spent most of that time talking to Doug. I was more focused on..." He trailed off, looking suddenly cautious despite his altered state.

"On your rock photography?" Nikki asked, smiling and making air quotes.

"Something like that." His smile wavered, the gummies clearly making him drowsy as his eyelids grew heavy.

"Tell me about your family," she said, strengthening her voice. "You mentioned earlier they were also into geology?"

"Yeah, my great grandfather was a miner. Spent months in these mountains prospecting. Left his family alone while he chased his dreams of striking it rich. My father and his dad were the same way. Said I was wasting time going to university when I could be out doing real fieldwork. They never had much respect for geologists who sat in offices."

"That must have been frustrating."

"Yeah." Ryan yawned, shifting against the log, trying to stay awake. "But they were right about fieldwork being where the real discoveries happen. And I'm not giving up on the annual assessment work. Have to make sure the claim stays in good standing. Marcus is helping. Says when we're ready to go public, everything has to be in order."

Nikki felt her eyes widen but gave a sage nod. "Sounds like important work."

"The most important work of my life," Ryan said then chuckled at his own seriousness. The gummies were taking over now. Moments later he gave up trying to stay awake, letting the drugs and mountain air lull him to sleep.

Watching him doze, Nikki wondered if Bear might not be involved with the mining operation. Ryan had left his geological equipment in his tent, suggesting he didn't trust Bear with his secret. That thought made her feel a bit better. But what was Doug's role?

Gunner's ears pricked and he gave a low whine. Familiar voices drifted across the meadow, giving Nikki enough time to scoop up Ryan's dope bag and return it to his tent. Then she grabbed a brush and circled around to the hobbled horses.

By the time the three hunters rode into camp, she was brushing Brownie while Ryan dozed against the log.

"How's our patient?" Bear asked, dismounting and glancing in Ryan's direction.

"Don't know," Nikki said, aware of Marcus stopping his horse beside Bear, waiting to hear her reply.

"I asked him about his ankle," she went on, "but he fell asleep before he answered. Guess he was tired from yesterday's festivities." She gave a tight smile, hoping the reference to last night might discourage Marcus from probing. She didn't want him to know she'd been questioning Ryan while he was under the influence.

There was also no need to expose Ryan's pain management techniques, or rather his boredom management. He was already the camp's whipping boy. And Marcus seemed determined to keep his friend from chatting too much. It made sense, now that she'd learned Marcus was involved in Ryan's mineral claim.

Bear's horse fidgeted, trying to sneak a bite of grass. Bear corrected him then led him toward the saddle rack. Thankfully Marcus followed. They seemed to accept her explanation, especially when the sound of Ryan's snoring drifted from the camp.

Soon, the returning horses were all untacked and grazing, and it was time to start supper. Bear gathered the food, Marcus lit the fire, and Doug juggled buckets as he headed toward the stream.

But even as Marcus praised the amount of kindling Nikki had gathered, she could only manage a polite smile, her thoughts consumed with what she'd learned: Ryan and Doug's presence on that old mining trail hadn't been an accident. Ryan was actively working a mining claim, likely with Marcus as his financial backer.

Yet the old claims couldn't be worth much. Gold, copper, and silver had been depleted decades ago. So what had Ryan discovered that was valuable enough to attract investors? Her mouth turned dry as the chilling possibility sank in—Elena had died because somehow she'd threatened their secret find.

CHAPTER TWENTY-ONE

The early morning air carried the bite of coming winter, turning their breath to visible puffs as Nikki stood holding Brownie's reins. Frost sparkled in the grass, catching the light like scattered coins, while the clear mountain peaks promised another beautiful day.

Bear stood beside her, watching Doug and Ryan ride away. The sound of hooves faded as the two men disappeared into a patch of trees.

"Miraculous recovery," Bear chuckled, shaking his head. "Ryan's ankle must be a lot better."

Nikki just nodded, adjusting her saddlebags that supposedly contained water sampling equipment. In reality, they only held the usual trail gear, but she was trying to keep that fact hidden. She'd also been careful not to leave anything personal in her tent. No ammunition, no ID, nothing that would reveal she was a licensed PI authorized to carry a weapon. Yesterday's search of Ryan's tent had reinforced how much one could learn from personal belongings.

"Likely Ryan can ride today because Doug's going to babysit him in the meadow while he takes his photography," Bear continued. "If they were really scouting game, that ankle would be too sore."

Nikki suspected that there wouldn't be any picture-taking and that once the two men were out of the trees, they'd swing their horses east and head up the old mining trail. And she intended to follow. She needed to find out if Ryan's grandfathered claim was valuable enough to justify murder.

"What kind of samples are you collecting today?" Bear asked, tugging his hat lower against the slanting sun.

"Have to check a bunch of locations for mineral content," Nikki said, patting her saddlebags as if the equipment inside was weighing on her mind. "When I called the office yesterday, they gave me some more testing protocols. Something about baseline readings before the hunting season impacts the watershed." She kept her explanation technical enough to sound legitimate but vague enough to avoid specific questions.

"I'd come and help, but I think it's best if I stay back with Marcus." Bear's voice lowered and he glanced toward the meadow where Marcus was circling the four remaining horses, rifle in hand, acting like a man on high alert.

"Yesterday I spotted those activists watching us from the cliff," Bear continued. "Didn't tell the others, but I'm worried about what Marcus would do if they try to sabotage our camp. He might fire some shots." Bear rubbed his jaw, the gesture betraying his unease. "And all hell could break loose after that."

Nikki cynically wondered if Marcus was acting hotheaded in order to keep a worried Bear in camp, leaving Doug and Ryan free to visit the claim. But the arrangement suited her. She needed to be alone to follow the two men.

She coiled her reins, eager to mount before Doug and Ryan got further ahead. She was certain they were heading toward the old mining trail where she'd found the horseshoe, but she didn't want to be left too far behind.

"Well, you be careful out there," Bear said, stepping back from Brownie. "Though I don't worry much about you. You're a good rider, and Brownie here is excellent at being alone. That's why I assign him to riders who want to do their own thing."

The mention of horses gave Nikki an opening she couldn't resist. "Do you always ride your buckskin?"

Bear laughed. "I only ride each horse for about two months. Once I'm sure a horse is trail safe, he's added to the client rotation. And I only use geldings. They're less complex."

"I imagine you have a few buckskins. They're known to be tough horses."

"They sure are," Bear said. "It's their black feet that make them good on rocks. They're also easy to recognize. Some of my clients can't tell a bay from a sorrel, but the buckskins and grays are easy to spot."

Nikki hid her frustration. Any of the men could have been riding with Elena on the day of her death. Her belief that it was Bear had just crumbled. But with that realization came a wave of relief. She'd grown to respect the guide. The thought of him being Elena's killer had weighed on her more than she'd realized.

And she couldn't ask any more questions. Bear was already looking at her with an odd expression. It didn't make sense for her to be fixated on something so unimportant as a horse's color.

"Well, I should get going," she said, swinging into the saddle. "Don't want to waste the daylight. Gunner!" she called.

He bounded over, tail wagging. She couldn't help but smile at his enthusiasm. This trip was the ultimate dog vacation. Away from the city's concrete, the choking smog and endless traffic, Gunner was in his element, tracking scents, alerting to danger, and roaming freely. And he also reminded her of something Sonja had said.

"Did Elena bring a dog on the spring trip?"

"A dog?" Bear's eyebrows drew together as he tried to process what Nikki was asking. "No, like I said earlier, we have a strict no-dog policy." Then he added, "Your dog is the exception, of course. If you manage to straighten out my insurance company, you and Gunner are welcome back anytime. You might prefer the fishing trips in September, seeing as you don't like guns."

Nikki adjusted the reins, not meeting Bear's gaze. It wasn't that she didn't like guns. She carried her own Glock and respected what firearms could do. But the careless way Marcus swung his rifle, treating it more like a prop than a deadly weapon, was alarming. Bear was also more astute than she'd given him credit for, picking up on her reaction. She wondered what else he'd noticed and whether her water story was as solid as she hoped.

The thought nagged at her as she rode away, but she forced herself to focus on what Bear had revealed. Any of the three men could have been riding a buckskin horse when Elena fell, but she was also less suspicious of Bear now that his clients seemed to be operating behind his back.

She purposely took a different route than the one Doug and Ryan had followed, but as she rode toward the trees, her neck prickled. She glanced over her shoulder. Bear had already moved on to splitting wood, but Marcus was watching her, rifle in hand.

The way he held his rifle, she wasn't sure he'd care about distinguishing between a dog and legitimate game. She had the unsettling urge to remove Gunner's orange vest, wondering if he might be safer without it.

The thought sent a chill down her spine. She moved Brownie sideways, putting herself between the dog and Marcus's line of sight. And her heart didn't slow its rapid pounding until they were protected by the trees.

CHAPTER TWENTY-TWO

Nikki followed Doug and Ryan's route, the dried valley grass crackling under Brownie's hooves. Gunner trotted ahead, nose down, though the crushed grass and fresh horse droppings made their trail easy to see. The smell of sage and decomposing oak leaves was cut by the calls of red-winged blackbirds, disturbed by their presence.

Morning shadows lay long across the meadow and she cut through a meandering creek, almost invisible in the tall grass. Seed heads brushed against Brownie's legs, releasing chaff that danced in the sunlight. His ears were pricked forward, sensing his buddies somewhere beyond the scattered oaks that dotted the valley.

The men had made a sharp turn once they reached the cliff, and Nikki gave a grim smile. Just as she'd suspected, they were heading toward the old mining trail. Gunner sniffed at a granite slab then turned onto the rocky trail. His tail gave a slight wag. Confirmation. The men had definitely gone this way.

She slowed Brownie's eager steps, not wanting to get too close. Horseshoes clicking on rock would carry. Worse, Brownie might nicker a greeting to Scout. She'd noticed how the two geldings called to each other whenever one returned from a ride, how they grazed side by side in the meadow, sometimes touching necks in companionship.

She considered taking another route, the one that led to the activists' first camp and then on to their cave. But that would risk leading the hunters to their hideout, and she didn't want to do that, considering Marcus's growing hostility.

Jake and Sage were likely watching right now. The caves offered a commanding vantage point, and they were highly motivated to disrupt the hunters. She wondered what they thought about riders climbing the mining trail. Did they think the men were coming after them?

Triplines were always a threat. Hopefully Doug was leading the way. He'd likely notice a trap but Ryan would be oblivious. He was more focused on rocks and mining claims than Scout's safety.

Brownie climbed eagerly, trying to catch up with his two buddies. She kept a wary eye on the ground but reasoned that Doug and Ryan's horses would hit any traps first. Still, the thought made her muscles twitchy. She hoped Sage had kept her promise not to set any more wires, and that she could curb Jake's more radical impulses.

The trail wound through stands of pine and fir where random boulders creating natural hiding spots. Stunted manzanita clung to rock crevices, their red bark bright against the weathered stone. Nikki kept a wary eye on the trees but caught no movement, either from the men or the activists.

Five minutes later, Gunner stopped and looked back, as if waiting for direction. At first she heard nothing, only the whisper of wind through pine needles. Then voices drifted from above, sharp and unmistakably male. She recognized Doug's voice mixed with Ryan's higher pitch, both men clearly agitated. Their words were indistinct, but the heated exchange carried. Whatever they'd discovered had triggered an argument between the two men.

Her heart beat faster. What would they say if they saw her? Her cover story about water sampling should work, but Bear had warned her to stay away from the cliffs. Of course, Doug and Ryan had no more business being here than she did. They'd told Bear they were going to photograph game in the valley.

The voices grew more irate. Brownie's head arched, ears pricked. He gave a low nicker, and she scrambled to the ground, quickly tapping his muzzle. She signaled for Gunner to heel then cautiously led Brownie further up the trail.

Once she rounded the bend, she could make out actual words. Doug and Ryan still weren't visible but the sound of their cursing was clear.

"Dammit," Doug said. "Sap is fresh. They must have cut it today."

Relief washed over Nikki. The activists had simply blocked the trail with a fallen tree, foregoing the more dangerous tripwires and showing consideration for the horses. But her relief was short-lived. If the trail was impassable, the men could appear at any moment.

She turned Brownie, positioning him for a quick getaway. But the grunting and swearing continued, joined with the sound of chipping wood, showing they were trying to move the tree. Clearly they didn't know about the alternate route.

So she waited, taking turns scratching Brownie's jaw and Gunner's ears, whispering praise for their patience. Brownie had obviously been on many hunts and was accustomed to standing silently for long periods. His black tail swished at a persistent fly, his eyes lowered. She no longer worried about him betraying her presence with an ill-timed whinny. And Gunner sat like a statue, his ears pricked toward the men, as if curious about their activities.

She fidgeted with the reins, accepting she was the most impatient member of their small party. The rhythmic chipping and crack of breaking branches suggested Doug and Ryan were making steady progress. What tools were they using? She doubted they carried a saw, so they were likely relying on smaller tools and brute strength to clear the heavier branches, exhausting work that would take time.

She led Brownie ten feet closer, straining to pick up more of their conversation.

"This will take hours to move," Ryan complained. "And they're watching all the time. What are we going to do?"

"There's only two of them," Doug said as the chipping sound stopped, showing he was doing the bulk of the cutting. "People disappear all the time."

The menace in his voice sent a chill down Nikki's spine, and she realized just how dangerous he could be. Every instinct screamed to turn around, ride back down the trail, and get away as fast as possible. But fleeing would only make her look guilty of something. She forced herself to take a steadying breath and ran through her water sampling story again, wishing she had actual test kits to make her cover more convincing.

How much would Doug believe? He'd already called her out for asking too many questions, his sharp legal mind picking up on inconsistencies that flew past the others. Of all the men, he seemed the most suspicious of her presence, the most likely to see through her excuses.

But this might be her only chance to figure out what they were doing. She was close enough to hear the rhythmic chipping of Doug's blade against wood and the crack of breaking branches. His instructions mixed with Ryan's labored breathing, along with the sharp, resinous scent of pine.

"We just need a few more samples," Ryan was saying, his words muffled by the sound of branches being dragged. "And pictures. Then you can file for incorporation. Is your contact ready?"

"Mining Division's just waiting on our paperwork," Doug replied. "Once we prove we've met the hundred-dollar minimum and have the documentation, they'll expedite the permits. Having someone inside helps."

"And Marcus has investors lined up?"

"Ready to pounce the second we go public." Doug's voice carried grim satisfaction between the scraping of his hatchet against wood. "Three-way split, just like we agreed."

Nikki sagged against Brownie's shoulder as the full scope of their plan hit. Mining in this pristine area could really happen. She tried to process the legal challenges. This had to be a grandfathered claim from the old mining era, and apparently the government would still allow extraction under certain circumstances.

But what could they have possibly found? The copper and silver deposits had played out. Gold was a remote possibility, but she couldn't imagine enough to justify this level of planning and investment. Regardless, if mining was allowed, this beautiful area could be destroyed. Equipment, access roads, extraction. Everything that made this place magical would disappear.

Her emotions were churning so much she almost missed Ryan's reply.

"Surveys confirm substantial deposits," he was saying. "Marcus says once we go public with the assay results, his investors will be fighting to buy shares." Ryan's voice turned dreamy, like it always did when he spoke about rocks, but now she didn't find it the least bit endearing.

She scrambled up on Brownie's back, fueled with urgency. She had to figure out what they were mining and where. But it was too risky following on their heels. Best to go back and take the other trail, the one that led past the activists' camp. If she moved fast, she could find a vantage point while they were cutting the tree. With all the old mines, it would be hard to find their claim without following. But after overhearing their casual talk of murder, she couldn't risk being discovered.

She still didn't know if one of the men was responsible for Elena's death but she'd certainly uncovered a motive. And men willing to kill to protect a lucrative mining scheme likely wouldn't hesitate to eliminate a second threat.

CHAPTER TWENTY-THREE

Nikki galloped Brownie across the grassland, determined to reach the mining area before the two men. Trees flashed past like sentinels and blackbirds scattered. Her hands gripped the reins as she leaned over Brownie's neck while Gunner ran beside them, tongue lolling but his gait effortless.

She slowed to a trot when the ground turned rocky, knowing she had to balance speed with safety. Fortunately, Brownie moved with confidence, familiar with the route she'd already taken twice.

They followed the base of the towering cliff, its shadows creating a corridor that chilled her face. The metallic ring of his shoes was alarmingly loud but soon they moved onto the portion of the trail carpeted with leaves.

They kept climbing, passing the tiny rivulet and its narrow granite chute. If she were truly collecting water samples, this would be a good spot, but she didn't have time to appreciate the sparkling cascade. She only stopped long enough for Brownie and Gunner to enjoy a cold drink, then pushed on.

Soon they reached the junction where she and Bear had left the main trail and followed Gunner to the activists' camp. The path wound through old stands of fir and cedar, forcing them to pick their way over fallen logs.

The clearing where the activists had camped looked the same. Totally empty. No olive-green tent, no camouflaged tarp, no scattered belongings. Gunner had already swerved onto the game trail and she followed, expecting this would be slower going. But Brownie kept his ground-covering walk, unfazed by the loose stone.

They reached the first scatterings of rusted mining equipment and she straightened in the saddle, watching Gunner, depending on him to alert to any scent. Judging by his behavior, she'd beat the men here and she gradually relaxed.

All she needed now was a safe place to tie Brownie. She heard the rushing waterfall but hesitated, reluctant to tie him in the activists' backyard. This was their living area and she was an intruder.

Gunner trotted around a boulder but quickly reappeared, as if wondering why she'd stopped. But she didn't want the activists to see her. Jake would doubtlessly untie her horse and that would leave her on foot. As well, Brownie could hurt himself if he galloped recklessly back to camp.

Probably best to lead him past the waterfall, find a secluded place to tie him, and hope that the sound of any nickers would be covered by the rushing water.

She dismounted and removed Gunner's orange safety vest. Then she loosened Brownie's cinch, and pulled a lead rope from her saddlebags. She also took her Glock, tucking the lightweight weapon into her jacket pocket. A check of her cell phone showed plenty of battery life for pictures, and she slipped her phone into the other pocket.

Gunner suddenly sat, tail wagging, and her throat went dry. His relaxed posture suggested someone familiar rather than threatening, but she still tensed, ready for confrontation.

"I hope you're not back here to use that gun on us?"

Sage stepped out from behind the boulder. The woman wore a thick fleece jacket that didn't hide the wary set of her shoulders. However her tone was more curious than hostile.

Nikki forced a smile, hoping Jake wasn't behind her. No way could she leave Brownie alone with him around. "Just wanted to check on two hunters from our camp," she said. "Wondering what they're doing up here and if anyone needs help..." She let her voice trail off, not wanting to say too much but hoping Sage might fill in some holes.

Maybe the activists had spotted something. They'd been watching the hunting camp long enough to know everyone's movements, and their position gave them a good view of the trails.

"Yes, Jake noticed recent mining work." Sage shook her head in disgust. "We saw two riders heading toward the old trail so we cut down a tree to stop them. What the hell is going on? First hunting, now mining?"

"I'm just as puzzled," Nikki said. "When I heard them trying to move the tree, I took the other trail. Wanted to get up here first. See where they go."

Sage stepped closer, her body relaxing. The mention of checking on hunters seemed to reassure her that Nikki was being responsible rather than threatening. "They were also up here two days ago," Sage said. "And it must be important if they made the effort to move the tree. It was a big one." Her gaze flickered over Brownie. "We didn't set any more trip wires. Jake and I discussed it, and neither of us want to hurt your horses."

Nikki felt a swell of relief, more confident about leaving Brownie. "Do you know where they're going? Is it in a cave?"

"Not sure, but Jake is hiding on the trail. If they get by that tree, he'll follow. Report whatever mining they're doing to Derek Stone. Then the coalition can raise hell."

"How does Jake plan to contact the office?" Nikki asked. When she'd checked her phone signal, she hadn't seen any bars, but maybe Sage knew a spot close by.

"He has a satellite phone. We can also access that ridge." Sage jabbed a thumb over her shoulder. "From here, it's only a thirty-minute hike. Usually there's cell coverage there."

"The ridge? The one where Elena fell?"

Sage nodded, and Nikki felt her stomach drop. "But those are dangerous men," she warned. "Jake shouldn't get too close. They might be involved in Elena's death."

Sage's face went through a series of expressions. Confusion, alarm, then growing denial. "I doubt those two hunters were even here in the spring," she said. "And Bear isn't with them. And neither of their horses is a buckskin." Her sentences ran together, as if saying the words fast would make them more believable. But her gaze hung on Nikki, as if seeking reassurance.

"Actually those two men were here in the spring," Nikki said, leading Brownie closer. "I'll try to warn Jake. Do you know a safe spot where I can tie my horse?"

"That tree behind those rocks. It's a white bark pine, one of the few that can handle this elevation. The root system goes deep."

Her expression darkened. "If they're really planning to reopen mining operations, the impact will be devastating. These streams feed into three different river systems, and the wildlife corridors…" She shook her head. "That's what Elena was checking. Do you really think those hunters killed her?"

"They were here the same time," Nikki said. "But I'm not sure about anything yet, other than they're more interested in this mining area than hunting. And that seems odd."

She paused, choosing her words. The last thing she wanted was to send Sage into a panic that might trigger a skirmish between the activists and hunters. Marcus was already itching for a fight, and Jake's earlier hostility showed he might welcome one as well.

"Look, I don't have proof of anything," she went on. "But there are too many coincidences. Elena was doing research in this area. Now these same men are working some kind of mining operation, and they want to keep it secret."

Sage's mouth tightened as her gaze swept the old sluices. "You can tell they used mercury amalgamation here. See how the soil has that grayish tint? Nothing grows there anymore. The watershed's still contaminated after all these decades. Maybe Elena found evidence of new pollution."

"Maybe," Nikki said. "But we have to be smart about this. Don't let Jake do anything to provoke a confrontation. They might have killed once before."

"But if they're illegally mining—"

"Then we gather evidence and let the authorities handle it," Nikki said. "That's why I rode up here. I can take pictures and make sure the right people see them. But Jake needs to stay back. And safe. That ridge has already claimed one life."

She watched Sage's face, seeing the conflict between environmental activism and personal safety. "I'm not asking you to quit your mission," Nikki added. "Just be careful how you go about it. These men have too much at stake to worry about another accident."

"I'll go with you to find Jake. To warn him."

"It'll be a bigger help if you stay here. If Jake comes back before me, you can explain things. Keep him calm." But Nikki could see the determined set of Sage's mouth and knew she needed a stronger argument.

"Plus, Brownie won't like being alone," she added, patting the gelding's warm neck. "He knows those two horses. If he starts whinnying, they'll call back. Then the men will know someone's around and might spot Jake. And they're already livid about the tree."

She lowered her voice, making her next point even more personal. "Frankly, if those men are killers, I don't want to be responsible for putting you in danger. You and Jake came here to protect the environment. Not to risk your lives. Let me do this part. If Marcus and Ryan see me, I can pretend I'm gathering water samples."

Sage turned, surveying the equipment scattered across the slope. Twisted cables snaked between rocks, their steel strands corroded to the color of dried blood. The skeletal remains of an ore cart lay on its side, wooden planks rotted away to leave only iron wheels and a rusted framework. A winch mechanism sat frozen in time, its gears seized by decades of neglect.

To their left, weathered timbers marked the entrances to several abandoned mine shafts, their openings staring like dead eyes. Thirty feet away, a faded sign warned of cave-ins and toxic gases, though some of the lettering had been scoured away by time and bullet holes.

Sage sighed. "They left such a mess. Before they figured out the environmental damage. But now there's no excuse." She turned back to Nikki, her expression troubled. "You really think they killed Elena?"

The question hung in the air, made more ominous by the graveyard around them, a testament to industrial ambition. Here, where men had torn apart the land in search of precious metals, it wasn't hard to imagine what people might do to protect a valuable discovery.

"I don't know," Nikki finally said. "But I think they're capable of killing."

Especially Doug and Marcus, she thought. And unfortunately, Doug was one of the men she had to follow.

CHAPTER TWENTY-FOUR

Nikki sprinted toward the mining trail with Gunner at her side, her breath forming puffs in the cold air. Fear and the thin atmosphere made her lungs work harder, but she was determined to reach the top before Doug and Ryan emerged. Without Brownie, she could move faster and stay hidden, and knowing Sage was watching the horse was a relief.

The rocky plateau offered little protection from the elements. Wind whistled through scattered debris, and clouds cast treacherous shadows over the ground. The temperature was dropping as a weather system approached, adding even more urgency.

She almost tripped over the remains of a sluice box, its planks bone gray and splitting, and slowed to a more reasonable pace. Getting injured up here would be disastrous. She motioned Gunner around a rusted cart wheel embedded in hardpan, wishing she'd thought to put on his protective boots. The terrain was a minefield of hazards for everyone.

Tailings piles surrounded them like burial mounds, and foundations showed where buildings had stood before collapsing beneath winter snow. Everywhere she looked, metal fragments and glass glinted among the rocks, any of which could slice open a dog's paw.

"Easy, boy," she whispered, keeping him by her side as they picked their way through the debris.

They were close enough now to see where the trail spilled onto the plateau. She spotted the perfect hiding place. A natural crevice between two massive boulders that gave an excellent vantage point. Once settled into position, she patted Gunner's head and strained to listen for the click of horseshoes that would announce the men's arrival.

She also watched for Jake but saw no sign of him. The area felt deserted, with only wildlife carrying on uninterrupted. A pika squeaked from a nearby rock pile where it was gathering winter stores, and a squirrel sat on an old wagon wheel, nibbling at a seed held between its tiny front paws. A flock of mountain chickadees moved through the stunted firs, their behavior suggesting no human disturbance.

Nikki checked her watch, wondering if the men had turned back. Maybe clearing that fallen tree had taken longer than expected. The sun set early at this elevation, and there were only a few hours of good light left. No one wanted to navigate these trails in darkness and Bear would be furious with that type of recklessness.

She was beginning to think it was time to return to the waterfall when Gunner stiffened beneath her hand. Moments later, she caught the clicking of horseshoes. It sounded like Doug and Ryan were riding fast, pushing their animals over the rocky ground.

They burst from the trail opening, close enough that she could see both horses had their ears pinned, irritated at the rough treatment. Ryan bounced in the saddle with each jarring step, but his face was creased in an excited smile. They maintained their pace, skirting a rusted winch and collapsed wooden chute as if familiar with the hazards.

When they disappeared behind a ridge of tailings, Nikki rose, signaling for Gunner to heel. She followed at a cautious distance, guided by the ringing horseshoes. With that much noise, she didn't need her dog's nose.

Fifteen minutes later, the sounds stopped. The men's voices became clearer, no longer muffled by distance. She crept forward, using boulders and scraggly vegetation for cover. Then she pulled in a deep breath and peered around the rocks.

Both horses were hobbled. Ryan was nowhere in sight, but Doug stood outside a cave entrance, scanning the surroundings with a sentinel's alertness. She pressed back against the rough granite. Did they somehow know she had followed?

Doug's vigilance certainly didn't extend to the horses. Scout had shuffled close to a crevice, and any horseman would have moved him to safer ground. But Doug's attention remained fixed on the approaches to the cave.

Nikki forced herself not to worry about Scout and instead studied the area. The rock formation was different from the common granite—dark greenish-black stone shot through with streaks that caught the light. She had no idea what type of rock it was, but the metallic veins running through it suggested mineral content.

Around the cave mouth, fresh chips and powder littered the ground while tool marks scarred the rock face. The strike of Ryan's hammer came from inside the cave. She itched to see what he was extracting, but Doug's position made a closer look impossible. Whatever they'd found here was clearly worth both the risk and secrecy.

She memorized the location and the approach routes, then eased back. Tomorrow was their final day of hunting, which meant the men would be out all day trying to fill their tags. She'd return here with plenty of time to document everything. Take photographs, maybe even collect a sample of that streaked rock for analysis.

Once out of earshot, she picked up the pace, jogging back toward Brownie. She needed to reach camp before Ryan and Doug returned, to be sitting innocently by the campfire when they arrived with their cover story about photography.

Sage met her at the waterfall, a huge trout in her hands that she was in the middle of cleaning. Blood and guts stained the water at her feet, and her hands were slick with the work.

"Did you find Jake?" Sage asked, gesturing at the collapsible bucket filled with fish bones. "I've been saving all the scraps. Jake insists we dump the bones and guts about a quarter mile away where the raccoons and coyotes can clean them up. It keeps the scavengers from getting too comfortable around our sleeping area."

"No sign of Jake," Nikki replied, catching her breath. "But he wouldn't be able to figure out what they're doing either. Doug's standing guard outside the cave where Ryan's working."

Sage gave a confident smile as she wiped her hands on a rag. "Jake knows routes around all these caves. He's an experienced climber. Bet he's watching Ryan right now from some ledge or crevice that Doug can't even see."

A chill ran down Nikki's spine. The confidence in Sage's voice only fueled her concern. "Those are dangerous men," she said. "Jake shouldn't go anywhere near that cave until they're gone."

Sage gave an absent nod, focused more on meal prep than Nikki's warning. She rinsed her knife and placed the cleaned fish in the natural cooling basin of the waterfall. "Do you happen to have another protein bar? I'd love to surprise him with dessert."

"There's a couple in my saddlebags," Nikki said, relieved Sage would have to admit to Jake that they'd been talking. At least that way Sage could pass on the warning about staying clear. As long as the activists avoided the hunters, they'd be safe. Bear's group would be riding out in two days, and then Jake could do whatever he wanted. Check out the cave, contact Derek Stone, organize the coalition.

Derek would be thrilled with any evidence they gathered. Nikki had seen how both Jake and Sage lit up whenever they mentioned their leader, how eager they were to prove themselves worthy. Jake especially seemed driven to impress Derek with bold action. Given his field experience, he might even be able to identify what Ryan was mining—the kind of breakthrough that would make Derek proud and cement Jake's standing within the coalition.

Nikki passed Sage the trail bars then mounted Brownie. She'd learned enough. For now, she needed to get back to camp before her absence raised questions. Tomorrow was their last full day, and she'd overheard Marcus and Doug saying they intended to bag a deer. Ryan might not be keen to hunt, but neither was he skilled enough to ride to the mining area alone.

That explained the men's urgency today, why they'd been so determined to move that tree and finish their mining work. She should be able to gather enough evidence to at least raise questions about their permits and the environmental impact.

But watching Sage's casual confidence as she bent to fillet the trout, Nikki couldn't shake her growing dread. She just hoped Jake would choose caution over heroics.

CHAPTER TWENTY-FIVE

Nikki sat by the campfire with Bear and Marcus, trying to ignore the ache in her lower back. The long day of riding followed by creeping around granite boulders had left her stiff and sore, made worse by her hurried ride back to camp as she'd tried to beat Doug and Ryan's return.

The oppressive weather matched her mood. Low-lying clouds had settled over the campsite, blocking the setting sun and casting everything in gray twilight. The heavy mist pressed down, muffling sounds and shrinking their world to the circle of firelight. Beyond that feeble glow, the mountains had vanished, and even the grazing horses were invisible.

Bear kept getting up, restlessly checking for any sign of returning riders. "Doug and Ryan should have been back by now," he muttered, glancing at his watch. "Sun's almost down, and those trails are no place to be riding in the dark. Especially with weather like this."

He paced around the campfire, scanning the trees. "Maybe I should saddle up and go look for them."

"Doug's very experienced," Marcus said. "I'm sure they'll be back any minute. You know how Ryan gets when he spots interesting geology. Probably lost track of time taking pictures.

Besides, we should talk about tomorrow's hunt. That trophy buck we spotted this afternoon—you're incredible at finding wildlife, Bear. Your tracking skills are what make these trips so successful."

Bear's expression brightened despite his worry. "That was a mature animal. Eight points, maybe more. If we get up early and position ourselves right, Ryan's new scope should help us spot him."

"Perfect way to end the trip," Marcus agreed. "Everyone goes home happy with a trophy like that."

Marcus turned to Nikki with a decisive nod. "You'll stay back tomorrow and watch the camp. Make sure those activists don't show up trying to mess with our horses."

Nikki nodded, noting how smoothly he'd shifted the conversation. And she had no intention of remaining in camp. Marcus obviously didn't want her riding around alone, but he couldn't know she'd already located the mining claim. Maybe he was worried she might stumble across one of Elena's missing trail cams. The thought sparked a burst of optimism.

The men would be gone all day hunting, and dressing a deer would slow their return even more. She also knew the activists wouldn't be visiting. They had their own agenda that didn't involve untying horses.

Bear frowned at Marcus. "There's no need for anyone to stay back. I'm taking the pack horses tomorrow with empty panniers. We'll need them if we're successful. Got to be ready to pack out the meat." His voice carried the edge of a man whose authority was being questioned. "So there will be no horses left in camp to protect."

The tension between guide and client was palpable. Marcus's jaw worked as if he were biting back words while Bear stood straighter, squaring his shoulders in the stance of someone who wouldn't be pushed around, even by paying customers. The silence stretched between them, heavy with an unspoken challenge.

"May I use the satellite phone to call my insurance office?" Nikki asked quickly, hoping to defuse the power struggle brewing between the two men. She really wanted to contact Justin and fill him in on everything she'd discovered, but her request might redirect their focus.

While she didn't completely trust Bear—he'd known his clients for years and could be involved in whatever they were hiding—she preferred him maintaining control of the camp. At least he followed professional protocols and was concerned about safety. Marcus, on the other hand, made decisions that likely aligned with the mining operation. And possibly something much darker.

"No point trying to call," Bear replied. "This cloud cover is too thick. No signal getting through tonight."

Nikki leaned forward and patted Gunner's head, drawing comfort from his steady presence. But she couldn't shake the realization that she was surrounded by potentially dangerous men with no way to call for help.

Gunner twisted, staring into the mist. Minutes later, hoofbeats sounded from the direction of the meadow. Bear hurried toward the riders, followed by Nikki and Marcus.

Ryan and Doug emerged from the shadows, their horses sweat-streaked but walking evenly. Both men were talking fast, clearly enthusiastic.

"Got some fantastic shots," Ryan called, gesturing at the heavy cloud cover. "The light in the valley was incredible. Those storm clouds created amazing contrast. The overcast conditions gave a moody, atmospheric quality you can't get with clear skies."

"Definitely worth being late for supper," Doug added. "And we had plenty of time to walk back and cool out the horses. Let them eat a little grass too."

Nikki listened to their coordinated story, impressed by how smoothly they delivered their lies. They'd rehearsed this explanation. "I'd love to see the pictures," she said, unable to resist.

Ryan flushed but Doug met her gaze, his stare icy cold. "Camera battery died," he said. "Shame you missed the show. Easy to do when people spend their time scrambling around the mountain streams instead of staying where they belong."

His voice carried an edge that made her stomach turn. Did he know she'd been up there? "Good thing I'm thorough," she said. "That's what the insurance company is paying for." She turned away from Doug, effectively ending the confrontation. "Let me help you with Scout," she offered Ryan, moving to his gelding's side.

Ryan slid from the saddle, nearly losing his balance as his boots hit the ground. "Thanks, Nikki. My ankle is a bit sore after the long day."

She loosened the cinch while Ryan chatted, still animated. "You should have seen the view from the valley floor. Definitely worth the ride. The way those peaks frame everything is like a picture."

His sheer enthusiasm made the lies easier to take than Doug's hostility. Even though she knew Ryan hadn't spent the day photographing the valley, his warmth was welcome. He seemed more like an excited tourist than a conspirator.

She unfastened his saddlebags, noting their bulging weight. Not surprising, considering what they contained. She moved to the other side of Scout, distracting Ryan with attentive nods while sliding her hand over the saddlebag. The leather was worn smooth, and she felt for an opening where she might slip out a rock sample. Ryan remained on the left side of the horse, still chatting about his great day, oblivious to her intentions.

"Ryan!" Marcus called from the end of the picket line. "Come settle an argument about that buck we saw."

As Ryan turned away, a dark shadow loomed over her, and she quickly moved her hand.

"I'll carry this to the tent," Doug said, reaching past her and pulling off the saddlebags. "Wouldn't want you to strain yourself after gathering all those samples."

She couldn't see his expression but the sarcasm in his voice was unmistakable, leaving her with the chilling possibility that Doug knew where she'd been today. Had he spotted her hiding among the boulders? Or was it his lawyer's instinct for deception that made him suspicious? The uncertainty was almost worse than knowing for sure that her cover was blown.

She had no desire to sit around the campfire tonight, where Doug's barbed threats would be waiting. The thought of pretending everything was normal while enduring his menacing attention left her knees weak. There was an intelligence behind those cold eyes that missed nothing. Worse was his cruel satisfaction when he made his comments, as if he enjoyed watching her squirm.

She spent the next half hour accompanying Bear, helping him feed and water the animals. She noticed he spent more time with Ryan and Doug's horses, even pulling out a flashlight to check their legs.

"Want me to hold the light?" she offered, still jumpy even though Doug and Marcus were over by the campfire. Her nerves were clamoring, as if danger was closing in.

"Thanks," Bear said, handing her the flashlight. "Just hold it steady. It's damn dark tonight."

He worked methodically, lifting Scout's left front first, then moving to the left hind. When he reached the right hind leg—the one where Scout had lost his shoe earlier—Nikki directed the beam closer.

"That new shoe looks worn for one day of valley riding," she said, angling the flashlight so the edge of its beam caught Bear's face, allowing her to gauge his reaction.

"Yup, shows some rocky ground." Bear set down Scout's foot and straightened, his eyes narrowing on the three men sitting by the fire. "Not the kind of terrain you'd find taking sunset pictures in the valley." His voice carried the concern of a professional guide who couldn't understand why his clients would lie about something so easily verified.

Nikki tightened her hold on the flashlight. Bear wasn't in on the mining operation. His confusion was genuine. But that knowledge didn't bring much comfort.

She was still surrounded by men hiding dangerous secrets, with no way to communicate with the outside world. Doug's relentless scrutiny made one thing clear. He was hunting her, and every instinct screamed that she was running out of time.

CHAPTER TWENTY-SIX

Nikki ran through darkness, her feet catching on loose rocks that sent her stumbling. Fear pounded through her chest as the monster pursuing her came closer with each step. She could hear it breathing behind her, feel its presence reaching out—

Something wet touched her face.

Shock jolted her awake, heart hammering against her ribs. For a disorienting moment she couldn't distinguish dream from reality. Then she felt Gunner's nose pushing against her cheek, his warmth against her skin. The air inside the tent was frigid, and she could see her breath forming pale clouds in the darkness. Her sleeping bag was twisted around her legs from thrashing during the nightmare, and she could feel the cold seeping through the thin nylon walls. The confines of her tent felt alien after the terror of her dream.

She lay motionless, steadying her racing heart, flooded with relief that it had only been a nightmare. Sweat beaded on her neck, and she wiped it away with a clammy hand. Had she cried out during the dream? The thought of Doug knowing she'd had a nightmare was infuriating. She didn't want to give him the satisfaction of knowing how deeply he scared her. Or how justified that fear had become.

But something had disturbed Gunner enough to wake her. He might have sensed her nightmare and wanted to comfort her, but his position by the tent door suggested there was something else.

His alert posture wasn't the warning he'd show if Marcus or Doug were prowling around, but he was definitely trying to tell her something.

She felt along the top of her sleeping bag until her hand found the familiar weight of her Glock. The cold metal was reassuring in her palm as she listened for whatever had caught Gunner's attention. The wind was too strong though, swirling through the camp and drowning out any sounds.

She pulled on her jacket, tucked the gun into her pocket, and followed Gunner from the tent. Then she stood close to the flap, straining to hear. The night was pitch black, thick clouds blocking the starlight, and the cutting wind made it tough to hear. Gusts whipped through the trees, and somewhere a branch creaked under the pressure. But these were normal sounds, the type of nighttime chorus that should have left Gunner sleeping peacefully.

She placed her hand on his shoulders, checking for raised hackles. His coat was smooth, his muscles relaxed. He wasn't alarmed, just focused as he stared toward the picket line. Whatever was out there was unusual, but not a threat.

"Heel," she whispered, keeping her hand on his shoulders, trusting him to guide her over the uneven ground.

The smell of horses reached her before she could see them. Then she made out Scout's pale hindquarters, a gray shadow against the night. Remembering how he'd kicked Gunner, she gave him a wide berth then paused behind the reliable Brownie. He was watching something on the other side of the picket line, curious but not fearful.

"It's me," a woman's voice whispered.

Sage. Nikki blinked with surprise then made her way around the horses, murmuring softly to keep them calm as she moved past. When she reached the front of the picket line, she spotted a gleaming pale oval. Sage's face was the only part of her visible.

"You shouldn't be here," Nikki said, checking over her shoulder. But she couldn't see the tents. Couldn't tell if anyone else was awake. She pulled Sage behind a large pine that offered some shelter from the cutting wind, though she kept her hand on Gunner, relying on him to alert her if any of the men approached.

"But it's about J-Jake. He never came back," Sage said. "Something's wrong. I didn't know what to do. I was hoping he was here, that maybe your hunters made him go with them..." Her words trailed off, carrying the desperate hope of someone clinging to unlikely possibilities.

Horror crashed over Nikki like a physical blow. Jake definitely wasn't here. She gulped, fighting the images of what might have happened. But there was no point in terrifying Sage further. Nikki had to focus on what could still be done.

Sage had already risked her life climbing down the mining trail in darkness and bitter cold. She must have navigated the rock and steep descent by feel alone, where one misstep could send her tumbling. True, she and Jake had made the climb down once before in the dark when they'd tried to free the horses, but it hadn't been this windy, and she hadn't been alone. The fact that Sage had come at all was a testament to her desperation.

Nikki could feel the woman's body shaking with cold and fear. Her face was pale even in the darkness, and when she reached out to clutch Nikki's hand, her fingers were icy.

"Listen to me," Nikki said, pulling off her jacket and wrapping it around Sage's shoulders. "You're going to sleep in my tent tonight. But we can't talk, and you have to be absolutely still. Can you do that?"

Sage gave a wordless nod, still clinging to Nikki's hand like a lifeline.

"The men will get up early to go hunting," Nikki continued, keeping her voice low. "Once they're gone, it'll just be you and me left in camp. We'll wait until they're well away, then head up to your cave. You'll stay safe there while Gunner and I search for Jake. Does that sound like a plan?"

"Yes," Sage whispered. "I'll do whatever you say. Please. Just find him."

"Gunner will track him," Nikki said, guiding Sage toward her tent, hoping they would make it through the next few hours without discovery. What she didn't say—what she grimly hoped—was that Jake would still be alive when Gunner found him.

CHAPTER TWENTY-SEVEN

The early morning air was still after the windy night, stars starting to fade in the eastern sky as Nikki studied Bear mounted on his horse. His worn leather chaps and faded jeans showed countless guiding trips, and his signature wide-brimmed cowboy hat tilted at the perfect angle. Everything about him spoke of competence, from his relaxed seat to the way he easily managed the lead ropes of two packhorses.

Her feelings about Bear had grown complicated over the past few days, but right now she just wanted him gone. The sooner the men rode out, the sooner she could help Sage search for Jake. Every minute they lingered increased the risk that someone would discover the terrified woman hiding in her tent.

And while she still couldn't completely rule out Bear's involvement in whatever his clients were hiding, she'd come to see him as one of the most trustworthy men in camp. His genuine confusion about the worn horseshoe, his concern for safety, and the way he followed protocol rather than bending to Marcus's demands all spoke to his integrity. If she had to trust anyone with her life, it would be Bear.

Doug, Ryan and Marcus waited on their horses, murmuring about their hunting plans while the animals' breath created clouds in the frigid air. Looking at the three men, a familiar knot twisted in Nikki's stomach. Doug remained the most threatening, his cold intelligence and calculating nature making her skin crawl. Marcus felt almost as dangerous with his need to control every situation and his casual talk of violence. Ryan, bouncing in his saddle with his usual energy, seemed like the odd man out. Too scattered and good natured to pose much of a threat beyond his terrible horsemanship.

"Even if the rack isn't what we hoped," Marcus was saying, "I'm ready to shoot any good-sized buck. My girlfriend has never eaten venison. I want to bring some home. Show her what she's been missing."

"Listen to the mighty hunter," Doug said, chuckling. "Next you'll be telling us about your prowess with a bow and arrow."

Bear leaned down, grabbing Nikki's attention. "Field dressing will take some time," he said, gesturing at the panniers on the pack horses. "If you decide to leave camp, stick to the east side of the valley. That area's safer for a solo rider."

Nikki nodded, shifting so she could see her tent where Sage was hiding. Gunner sat by the zippered flap, tail wagging, eager to return to their unexpected guest. She motioned him to her side, relieved that none of the men had picked up on her dog's behavior.

But the back of her neck was prickling and she caught Doug watching Gunner as he trotted to her side. Even in the dim light, Doug's attention seemed menacing, and she placed a protective hand on her dog's head. Her other hand brushed against the Glock still tucked in her jacket pocket from last night, and she found herself calculating distances, angles, how quickly she could draw if Doug made any move toward her partner. The possibility of anyone threatening Gunner awakened something cold and lethal in her chest. She held Doug's stare with unflinching intensity, letting him see exactly what kind of enemy he'd make if he touched her dog.

Doug gave a mocking nod before turning his attention back to Marcus, who was discussing the best way to fry venison. Their dismissive attitude no longer bothered her—in fact, she was grateful they'd missed the steel in her eyes, the way her hand had moved instinctively toward her weapon. Let them think she was someone who'd stay meekly in camp, content to tend the fire. Their assumptions about her limitations could be her biggest advantage.

It was a relief when the men finally rode off, their horses' hooves muffled by the frost-tipped grass. Bear said something and conversation ceased. He obviously knew Marcus wanted to shoot his deer, and this was a serious hunt. Brownie gave a plaintive nicker from the picket line, wondering why he was the only horse being left behind.

Nikki waited until the men were out of sight. Then she jogged back to her tent and unzipped the flap.

Sage sat cross-legged, fully dressed and waiting. Dark circles ringed her eyes, and her blonde hair hung limp. She looked exhausted, like someone who'd spent the entire night worrying.

"They're gone," Nikki said. "It's safe to come out."

Sage crawled from the tent and straightened slowly, one hand pressed to her lower back. She took careful, short steps as if her legs had cramped from being folded too long in the cold. The physical toll of her grueling descent down the mountain was obvious, though she tried to hide it.

Nikki led Sage to the campfire and poured her coffee from the warm pot left on the grill. Working quickly, she grabbed two thick camp buns and looked questioningly at Sage. "Are you vegetarian? I can make peanut butter and jam, or there's meat and cheese."

"Peanut butter and jam is perfect," Sage said, with a weak smile.

Nikki slathered the buns with thick layers of peanut butter and jam, then watched as Sage devoured both of them so quickly it made Nikki wince. Clearly, the young woman was famished.

"Take your time," Nikki said, understanding the gnawing worry that was driving Sage. "We'll leave in about ten minutes."

She retrieved her saddlebags from the tent and headed to the picket line to groom and saddle Brownie. Sage followed, coffee cup in hand, her impatience to begin the search evident despite Nikki's advice to slow down.

"I keep thinking he might have fallen and broken a leg or something," Sage said, her voice tight with anxiety. "Maybe he's lying somewhere hurt, unable to get back to the cave."

Nikki's heart ached at the hope in Sage's voice. "Did he have a satellite phone with him?"

"Yes, in his pack. Standard equipment when we're in the field."

"Maybe he called your coalition office," Nikki said. She strode to Bear's tent and peered in, on the slim chance he might have left his phone. But she only saw his personal gear. No satellite phone.

The possibility that Jake had already contacted someone offered a glimmer of hope, though Nikki couldn't shake her dread. She did not want Sage with her during the search. If Jake was dead—and her gut told her that was increasingly likely—Sage shouldn't be the one to find him. The woman had already endured the trauma of seeing Elena's crushed body at the bottom of that cliff. Finding Jake's corpse would be devastating enough without having witnessed it firsthand. Some images burned into memory forever, and she wanted to spare Sage that particular nightmare.

"I'll ride ahead," she began, but Sage shook her head.

"I can keep up with your horse," Sage said. "We do it all the time when we're following hunters. Jake and I can jog for miles behind riders without them even knowing we're there."

Nikki saw the determination in Sage's face and knew the woman would dig deep to keep up. But she'd be drawing on already depleted energy. No way was Nikki going to let her jog beside Brownie. "We'll ride double on the flat ground," she said. "Save your energy for the climb."

She moved the saddlebags to the front of the saddle, attaching them to the D-rings. The setup was bulky but manageable. She mounted first then pulled Sage up behind her. Brownie accepted the second passenger as if he'd been ridden double before, and Nikki felt a wave of gratitude. Some horses would have thrown a bucking fit.

The sun was peeking over the horizon when they headed out. Light touched the mountain peaks while shadows retreated across the valley floor. The grass sparkled and the crisp air warmed with the rising sun. It would have been a beautiful morning if Nikki could only shake her apprehension.

"I can't believe this is happening," Sage said, her voice close to Nikki's ear. "Jake is so careful about everything. He's the one who taught me wilderness safety, how to read weather, how to move quietly through the woods."

"How did you two meet?" Nikki asked, hoping conversation would keep Sage distracted.

"At a climate protest in Sacramento. I was handling media relations for the event—that's my background, public relations. Jake was one of the speakers, and he was so passionate about protecting the wilderness." Sage's voice warmed with the memory. "We've been together about six months. He got me connected with

Derek Stone's coalition. My goal is to become an environmental influencer, use social media to raise awareness about conservation issues."

"That's important work," Nikki said, guiding Brownie around a patch of loose rock.

"Jake thinks we can truly make a difference. He says every wilderness area we save is a victory for future generations." Sage's arms tightened around Nikki's waist. "We share the same values. The same vision for what the world could be."

When they reached the mining trail, both of them dismounted. Nikki didn't want Brownie carrying double weight up the steep incline, especially when one of the riders was sitting behind the saddle, restricting his hind end.

"We'll walk on opposite sides," she said, "each with one hand on a stirrup. Let him help us."

They climbed steadily, using Brownie's solid presence for support. When they reached the big tree that Sage and Jake had felled the day before, Nikki paused to examine it.

The trunk was two feet in diameter, requiring serious effort to bring down. She could see the deep cuts on both sides where Sage and Jake had worked with what must have been a folding saw, and the fresh wood chips scattered around showed where Ryan and Doug had used a hatchet.

"This would have taken a while for you to cut," Nikki said.

"Yes." Sage gave a glimmer of a smile. "Jake wanted to make sure we'd block the horses."

But they hadn't, Nikki thought. Ryan and Doug weren't going to be stopped by a mere tree. They scouted around the adjacent trees, calling Jake's name. But there was no sign that he was nearby and Gunner showed little interest.

So they pressed on until they reached the waterfall, its cascade creating a cool mist that felt refreshing after the climb. Nikki removed Brownie's saddle and bridle, gave him a chance to drink, then tied him to the same sturdy pine they'd used the day before. She rummaged through her saddlebags, transferring everything else she might need to her jacket pockets—her phone, plastic scent bag, bear spray, extra ammunition. Her Glock was already there, where she'd been keeping it close since learning Jake was missing.

"Nikki!" Sage called impatiently. "This way."

She led Nikki behind the waterfall and through the narrow opening. "Jake found this place," she added with obvious pride. "It's perfect for watching the hunters without being seen."

Her voice carried the satisfaction of someone who appreciated both the security and strategic value of their hidden camp.

The cavern was larger than Nikki had expected, connecting to an even bigger chamber beyond. Jake and Sage had created a minimalist camp with sleeping bags spread on flat rocks, food supplies in waterproof containers, and basic camping gear. Cell phones sat beside a small solar panel, though Sage explained the phones only worked when carried up to the ridge.

"We have an incredible view," Sage said, "It's even better than our last campsite." She scooped up the solar panel and led Nikki to the cave mouth where she positioned the panel then connected her cell phone to charge. "With this weather clearing up, we should have full power soon."

The vantage point was spectacular, offering a sweeping vista of the entire valley. Nikki could see the cliff where Elena had fallen, the wilderness areas beyond normal reach, and multiple escape routes through the rocks.

"Are you comfortable going up to the ridge and trying to call Jake's satellite phone?" Nikki asked. "If he's injured somewhere, he might answer."

Sage's face brightened, hope flickering in her tired eyes. "Yes! I should have thought of that earlier. But please wait so I can help look for him."

"I don't want to lose any more time," Nikki said. "Every minute matters if he's hurt. It's best if you try calling from the ridge, then come back here and wait. If Jake makes his way to the cave, you'll be here for him."

Sage hesitated, clearly torn between wanting to search and understanding Nikki's logic.

"I need something of Jake's," Nikki said, pushing her advantage. "Clothing with a strong scent."

Sage disappeared into the cave and returned with a pair of crumpled boxer briefs. "How about these?" she asked. "They're a little dirty. We haven't washed them yet."

"Perfect," Nikki said, pulling a plastic bag from her pocket. As she deposited the briefs, she glimpsed the spotted fawns scattered across the underwear. The decoration made Jake seem younger, and tugged at her heart.

She had to swallow before speaking again. "I'll take Gunner back to the other side of the waterfall and work from there. You try reaching Jake with the phone. Also call your office. See if they've heard from him. I'll meet you back here."

She headed for the waterfall, fighting her growing certainty that twenty-four hours in these mountains might already be too long. Last night the temperature had dropped near freezing, and if he was injured and exposed to the elements, hypothermia could have set in.

If Jake was still alive, she had to find him soon.

CHAPTER TWENTY-EIGHT

Nikki scanned the top of the mining trail where it opened onto the familiar rocky plateau. The area looked much the same. Weathered sluice boxes, rusted wheels, and stone foundations marked where buildings had once stood. Jake had likely followed Ryan and Doug up the trail and she hoped Gunner would pick up his scent without backtracking further.

Right now, Gunner trotted in ever-widening circles, nose working as he searched. Scent didn't hold on granite the way it clung to vegetation and soil, and the rocky surface made his job more challenging. He'd have better success picking up the scent where Jake might have brushed against bushes or stepped on patches of earth.

She considered directing him into the woods where Jake's scent might be stronger. But within minutes, Gunner's behavior changed. His tail lifted and he straightened toward the boulders, only twenty feet from the route she'd watched the horses take yesterday.

She stuffed the scent bag in her pocket and hurried after her dog. Jake had been cautious, skirting the direct path and staying roughly a hundred feet from the mining cave. His route wound between granite boulders and stunted vegetation, offering plenty of cover. But he wasn't going in the right direction. Maybe he'd lost sight of the men and been unable to find them.

But that didn't make sense. Their horses' shoes had clicked on the rock. Jake could have easily tracked the sound. And according to Sage, he'd spent considerable time exploring and was an experienced caver who knew the terrain. It seemed unlikely he'd been confused about where the men had gone.

But Gunner remained intent on the trail and she trusted his instincts. Maybe Jake had made the same decision she had—that it was too dangerous to get close while Doug stood guard. The activists' cave wasn't far away and from their vantage point they had a view of the valley. He must have decided to wait until Ryan and Doug were off the mountain.

She blew out a sigh of relief. In remote areas, caution kept people alive, and though Jake had struck her as headstrong, he was clearly experienced enough to prioritize safety. Since they were quite far from the cave where Doug and Ryan had been working, maybe he'd simply fallen.

"Jake!" she called, hoping he might answer from somewhere among the rocks. Perhaps he'd broken a leg and was helpless, unable to make it back to camp.

But there was no answer and Gunner kept leading her deeper through a maze of rocks and brush. The terrain opened up, offering a view of the inaccessible valley below, wild timber country where few humans ventured. Game trails crisscrossed the area in complex patterns before disappearing onto bare rock.

Gunner slowed to sniff at a brownish-green clump, then continued forward with renewed purpose. When he paused again a few feet ahead, something caught Nikki's eye. A small square box camouflaged within the brush. She might never have spotted it if Gunner hadn't drawn her attention.

A trail camera. And it bore the university logo.

"Wait," she instructed Gunner, her pulse quickening as she reached out to unfasten the camera. Elena had positioned it well, monitoring the game trail and a small rocky pool where animals came to drink. Nikki checked the display but the battery was dead. The cold mountain nights had taken their toll.

She stuffed the camera into her jacket pocket. Bear might have replacement batteries back at camp. He likely used trail cams to monitor game. And if not, the recordings could wait until she returned to her office. The university would want Elena's research data. The biologist had lost her life documenting water and wildlife patterns. Her unfinished work deserved to be completed.

Nikki encouraged Gunner forward, aware that stopping him could disrupt his focus. But he continued on, leading her to a cluster of manzanita bushes with twisted red branches and sharp thorns that caught at her jacket. The hardy shrubs grew in thin soil between the rocks, their small waxy leaves offering minimal cover.

Gunner rounded the bushes, following Jake's trail then vanished. Nikki blinked, then realized the brush concealed a dark cave entrance, almost invisible unless one knew where to look.

She pulled out her phone and activated the flashlight, realization dawning. Jake had found a back entrance to the mining cave. She felt a surge of respect for his wilderness skills, followed immediately by dread.

Her stomach knotted as she stared into the opening. Gunner was focused on the cave, showing no interest in any exit route. That meant Jake hadn't come out. Whatever had happened had occurred in the suffocating darkness beyond her light beam. Everything in her rebelled against entering that black void, but she couldn't stop now. She'd promised Sage she'd find him.

"Gunner," she called. He reappeared, looking impatient at another delay. But she clipped on his leash, knowing the rock floor could be treacherous. Limestone caves were notorious for sudden drop-offs where underground water had carved away the stone, creating sinkholes and fissures that could swallow a person without warning. She wasn't about to lose her dog to the same hazards that might have claimed Jake.

The cave entrance was narrow, forcing her to duck. Water dripped from the ceiling, creating a slippery floor that made each step treacherous. Something scurried beyond her light beam—bats or rodents disturbed by their presence. The air was stagnant, carrying the musty smell of damp rock and centuries of mineral deposits.

Her boots sounded loud in the confined space, and she found herself holding her breath, trying to minimize any noise. A few yards in, the floor simply vanished. She stopped just short of a yawning crevice, the beam of her phone revealing nothing but blackness.

"Jesus," she whispered, her sweaty hands tightening around Gunner's leash as she swallowed her fear. The crevice cut straight across the passage, but there were a few feet of solid rock on either side where the cave floor remained intact. They gingerly skirted the dangerous gap, staying close to the wall where the footing was secure, and pressed on through the claustrophobic passage. The ceiling forced her to crouch awkwardly, her back aching as she duck-walked beside Gunner.

Gradually, the air became fresher and the passage widened enough for her to straighten. Daylight filtered in from ahead, and she spotted the opening to the main chamber where Ryan had been working. The cave was connecting just as Jake seemed to have known.

She ran her light over the walls. They showed the same dark greenish-black stone shot through with metallic veins. Tool marks scarred the surface. But Gunner whined and strained at his leash, clearly wanting to continue.

He led her down a tunnel where a maze of passages fanned out from the main chamber. She was reluctant to go too deep without proper equipment—ropes, headlamps, and safety gear—but Gunner's head was up, working air scent now. The cave floor was rough, but at least there were no more hidden holes. And only fifteen feet in, he stopped and sat, his signal for a find.

They'd reached a section where the passage simply ended, opening into a vertical shaft that dropped into darkness.

Her heart hammered as she gripped her phone and inched forward. The beam revealed a narrow shaft, with a drop of about thirty feet, maybe more.

She panned her light around the rocky floor. Something orange caught her eye. A satellite phone, its bright case stark against the gray stone. And then she saw the pale shape of a hand, fingers curled in the stillness of death.

Jake's body lay crumpled at the bottom of the pit.

Beady eyes glowed in her light before scurrying into the darkness. The sight of the fleeing rats hit her like a gut punch, confirming her worst fears. She sank to her knees, fighting a wave of grief. Jake had been passionate about protecting the wilderness. Now she'd have to return to Sage with the devastating news that her boyfriend was never coming home.

But first, she had to steel herself and gather evidence. She needed photographs of the scene and rock samples from the main chamber. Whatever had happened here—accident or murder—Jake deserved justice. And Sage deserved the truth.

CHAPTER TWENTY-NINE

Nikki knelt on the rough cave floor, groping around the area where Ryan had been hammering. Her phone battery was dying, the screen flickering weakly before going dark. She couldn't even take pictures now. Working by touch, she felt for the small cuttings and chips that would have scattered when Ryan's geological hammer struck the wall.

Her fingers found several pieces, some no larger than pebbles, others the size of her thumb. Even in the low light filtering from the entrance, color flashed in the samples, metallic flecks that seemed to shimmer with an inner fire. These fragments might show why their discovery had left Ryan so excited.

And she needed to get out. The dark chamber pressed around her like a tomb. Caves were deceptive labyrinths where explorers could lose their way, wandering in circles until their lights failed. She'd read about cavers found years later, their bodies curled mere yards from safety, victims of a single wrong turn.

The thought drove her forward, following Gunner and the growing light that promised escape. At least they didn't need to retrace their path through that maze of passages. This route led straight to the opening where Doug had stood yesterday. Just ahead, daylight beckoned. Each step brought her closer to freedom, but also closer to the devastating conversation awaiting her with Sage. Soon she'd need to tell the young woman that Jake's body lay broken at the bottom of a shaft.

The local sheriff's department would coordinate the recovery, but that would require mountain rescue teams and could take days to organize. The faster they were notified the better. It would be quicker to climb the ridge and make the call with Sage's solar-charged phone than return to Bear's camp and wait for his return from the hunt.

Nikki burst from the cave, the daylight on her face a welcome relief after the suffocating darkness. The mining area stretched around her, littered with rusted equipment and collapsed wooden structures from a bygone era. And it seemed the men wanted to renew extraction.

She stepped over a jagged cable, its metal fragments catching the afternoon sun like broken glass. But Gunner's growl made her jerk up. His ears were pricked, hackles rising, as he stared at something beyond an overturned ore cart.

She followed his gaze, her breath catching. Doug sat on his horse only twenty feet away, silently staring like she was a deer framed in his crosshairs. His horse was sweat-streaked, its flanks heaving.

Finally Doug spoke. "Thought I'd find you here."

Nikki forced her expression to remain calm, though her skin felt as if insects were marching across her shoulders. "Just gathering the last of the water samples," she said, relieved that her voice sounded steady. "Did Marcus get his deer?"

"Don't know. Don't care." The dismissive words revealed that his visit this fall had nothing to do with hunting. "And cut the bullshit about water samples. Empty your pockets. Now."

Nikki could see Doug's eyes fixed on the bulges in her jacket pockets. Better to reveal the rock samples willingly than have him demand to see everything she was carrying. If she pulled out the mineral fragments, maybe she could keep her other hand positioned to hide the outline of her Glock. She reached into her jacket pockets and pulled out the rock fragments, while keeping her left side angled away from his view.

Doug's face went white as he stared at the evidence in her hands, then flushed an ugly red. "I knew it!" he spat, his voice choked with rage. "You have no idea what you're messing with."

"It's just some rocks," Nikki said, trying to sound confused. "I thought maybe Elena was looking for gold or something. You know, old mining claims up here."

Doug's laugh was bitter. "Gold? You think this is about some played-out gold mine?" His voice rose with each word. "This isn't some penny-ante claim that's been picked over for a century. It's enough rare earth minerals to fund early retirement."

Nikki forced her expression to remain blank, as if she had no idea what rare earth minerals were or why they mattered. "I don't understand—"

"Of course you don't!" Doug's professional frustration poured out in a torrent. "I've spent twenty years kissing ass, watching junior partners get promoted over me while I did their work. Twenty years of being passed over, overlooked, undervalued." His hands clenched into fists. "This is my shot. And I'm not letting any bleeding hearts destroy it."

His horse shuffled beneath him, responding to its rider's fury. Doug's voice hardened as he yanked viciously on the reins. "Guess it's time for you to join your activist friend."

The words slammed into her like ice water. He wasn't making threats. He was confessing to Jake's murder, and clearly didn't intend to let her leave. She gulped. There'd be no talking her way out of this, not by words or deflection.

Nikki's mind raced. Her Glock was no match for a hunting rifle. The scattered mining equipment offered poor cover against a weapon designed to drop big game. And Gunner was equally exposed.

She spun, calling her dog even as she bolted toward the cave entrance. "Gunner, come!"

The first gunshot cracked. Rock exploded inches from her head, granite fragments peppering her cheek. She zigzagged as the second shot rang out, the bullet whining off an ore cart with a metallic shriek.

She vaulted over a twisted steel cable, her heart hammering. Leaped across a narrow trench, rocks sliding treacherously beneath her feet. She could hear the horse spooking from the gunfire. Doug cursed, still working the bolt action. Its metallic click promised death if she stumbled.

Ten more feet. And no bullet had hit them yet. Then she plunged into the blessed darkness of the cave, Gunner beside her. The temperature dropped ten degrees, wrapping around her like a cool embrace. She stumbled deeper into the passage, her hands pressing against the walls for guidance.

Hoofbeats approached outside. Then stopped. She could hear the rustling of saddlebags, guessed Doug was pulling out the hobbles, gathering a flashlight. So he was leaving his horse and following her in.

She pressed back against the rough wall, determined not to give away her location. The rocky chamber amplified every sound. Her heartbeat, Gunner's panting, the subtle shift of her boots. But the cave also offered protection. Bought her time to think. To mentally map the cave system.

This main chamber stretched about twenty feet deep before branching into three small passages. But beyond those lay a confusing labyrinth of interconnected passages, some no wider than her shoulders, others splitting again into multiple routes that might stretch into the mountain's heart. She'd never have found her way to Jake's body without Gunner's nose leading the way.

And her small phone light had only revealed a fraction of the cave system: glimpses of side tunnels and crevices that disappeared into black voids. Now, with no light at all, feeling her way through this maze would be suicide. One wrong turn and she could wander for hours, stumbling into dead ends or worse, vertical drops that would send her plummeting into the darkness.

But if Gunner could retrace their earlier path, he might be able to guide her through the maze and to the back entrance Jake had found. She just had to find a way to let Gunner know what she wanted.

And she'd watch for a chance to take a shot. Doug didn't know she had a gun. But the problem was her complete lack of light. In this pitch black darkness, she'd have to wait until he was close enough that she couldn't miss—point-blank range. Otherwise, he'd mow her and Gunner down with that rifle. She'd have one opportunity, and her shot would have to be perfect.

Doug might be better equipped yet she had advantages too. Gunner and the element of surprise. And somewhere in this maze of passages, she'd find a way to make both count.

CHAPTER THIRTY

Nikki pulled her Glock from her jacket, the weight steadying her shaky hand. She crouched behind an outcrop, pressing against the cave wall as darkness wrapped around her like a curtain. The musty air was thick with the smell of minerals and wet rock, the cold seeping into her bones.

She strained to see, watching for the first glimpse of Doug's flashlight. The blackness was so complete it had physical weight, pressing against her eyeballs until she couldn't tell if they were open or closed. Her mouth had gone dry, and adrenaline made every nerve ending crackle with awareness.

She groped in the darkness with her other hand, searching for Gunner's warm body. Could feel the vibration of a growl building in his chest. She tapped his nose with a finger, their signal for silence. His growl stopped, though she could feel his body coiled with tension, every muscle ready to spring.

A subtle shift in the air made her freeze. Then she caught it, a faint glimmer dancing off the walls. Doug was coming, moving with confidence through the chamber. He clearly knew this area well, probably had explored every adjoining passage, checking the formations.

What kind of minerals could be valuable enough to make murder so acceptable? The question flickered through her mind before urgency pushed it away. She had to move. Now.

"Home," she whispered to Gunner, the word barely audible. She prayed he'd understand, that he'd lead her to the back entrance where they'd first entered this maze. Not to Jake's body. And not into a premature confrontation with an armed killer.

She placed one hand on his shoulder and gripped her Glock in the other, then stepped away from the wall. Without that stone guide, she was completely dependent on her dog. Each step had to be deliberate, careful not to kick loose rocks that would reveal their position.

The darkness was disorienting, affecting even her balance. She felt like she was floating in black space, tethered only by Gunner's steady movement beneath her hand. She could hear Doug's confident footsteps and occasional glimpses of light as it bounced off distant walls.

Gunner moved slowly, cautiously. Dogs had better night vision than humans, but in this absolute darkness even his abilities were limited. She hoped he could smell their trail from earlier, though scent didn't hold well on bare rock, and each blind step felt like a leap of faith.

Doug's voice suddenly echoed through the cave system, distorted and multiplied by the stone passages. "It's better to let me shoot you than get lost in here and starve!" His laughter reverberated through the tunnels, growing more unhinged with each echo, the sound seeming to come from everywhere at once.

Her gun shook in her grip. She released Gunner and slid her hand along the wall, desperately searching for a crevice where they could hide until Doug passed, then ambush him. But the stone was solid, offering no sanctuary. Frustration burned in her chest. She was helpless, stumbling blind while a predator who savored stalking his prey closed in.

Seconds later the light disappeared. Not even a glimmer. She pulled in a shaky breath, hoping Doug had taken a different passage. Maybe they'd lost him in the labyrinth.

But minutes later, the light was back. Moving even faster.

"Bitch!" Doug's enraged voice carried through the tunnels. He must have taken a wrong turn, wasted time, and now he was making up ground with savage fury.

Gunner picked up his pace, pulling her along as if sensing the urgency. His movement was more purposeful now, and she felt a cool breeze touch her face. They rounded a corner and she was nearly blinded by light streaming into the tunnel.

The opening looked like where they'd entered earlier. Same size, similar angle of afternoon sunlight. Relief flooded through her and she hurried toward the promise of escape.

But Gunner suddenly blocked her path. She stumbled to a stop, confused by his behavior until she looked past him and her heart nearly stopped. The crevice yawned directly ahead. A black gap in the cave floor that would have swallowed her if she'd taken two more steps.

"Good boy," she whispered, her voice shaking. If Gunner hadn't stopped her, if she'd rushed when Doug's taunts made her panic, she would have fallen into that abyss. The thought made her stomach lurch.

They gingerly skirted the crevice, Nikki keeping a firm grip on Gunner's collar. Once past the deadly fissure, they hurried toward the cave opening where she pushed Gunner outside. "Stay," she commanded, then edged back into the cave's entrance.

She flattened against the cave wall, raised her Glock and aimed at the spot where Doug would emerge. She had to make the shot. He wouldn't be as blinded as she'd been. His flashlight had given his eyes some preparation for brightness, but the streaming sunlight would still create a contrast that required adjustment.

And if he was hurrying, those seconds of disorientation might be all she needed. The transition from artificial light to daylight might throw him off, especially if anger made him reckless.

Doug's steps grew louder, more confident. "There's no place to hide," he called, and she could hear the cruel satisfaction in his tone as he savored her helplessness. "Let's make this quick so I can get back and see Marcus's deer."

The casual dismissal sparked a surge of rage. Jake was dead—murdered for trying to protect the environment he loved—and Doug was treating it like a minor inconvenience before returning to his hunting vacation. The callous indifference to a young man's life made her blood boil.

The rage burned away her reluctance to shoot without warning. This wasn't some petty criminal she might reason with. This was a killer who'd thrown Jake's body into a pit like garbage and likely pushed Elena off that cliff. Her finger tightened on the trigger as fury replaced hesitation. Doug had forfeited his right to mercy the moment he decided human lives were worth less than mining profits.

Yet even through her anger, tactical awareness kicked in. His hunting rifle had range and power that her Glock couldn't match. She'd seen him handle weapons with practiced ease around camp. She needed to draw him into rushing forward, make him abandon the advantages his superior firepower gave.

"Guess they were right not to make you partner," she called, her voice steady despite her hammering pulse.

"You don't know anything about my career!" Doug snarled. "I earned a partnership!"

She could see the glow of his flashlight now, bouncing wildly as he charged toward the opening. He burst into the light with his rifle raised, eyes squinting against the sudden brightness, just as she'd hoped.

He never saw the crevice.

One moment he was silhouetted in the light, and the next he was gone. His scream cut off, replaced by a distant thud. The flashlight beam spun wildly before vanishing into the depths, followed by a metallic clatter.

Nikki's arm went weak as she lowered her weapon. The silence returned, broken only by the whisper of wind and Gunner's whine. It was over. Jake's killer would never hurt anyone again, claimed by the same wilderness he'd violated.

She turned toward Gunner, poised inside the cave. He hadn't listened to her 'stay' command. He was a dog who sometimes made his own decisions. His grave expression held an intelligence that went beyond training. He'd understood the life-or-death stakes and had been ready to charge between her and danger, regardless of the cost.

Throughout this nightmare, he'd guided her through that dark maze, stayed silent when discovery meant death, and positioned himself to defend her even when ordered away. Some partnerships transcended simple commands.

He trotted to her side, his solid presence a reminder that she wasn't alone. They'd survived this together, but their ordeal wasn't over. Now came perhaps the hardest part—breaking the devastating news to Sage.

# CHAPTER THIRTY-ONE

Nikki sagged against a boulder outside the cave entrance, trying to settle her emotions. Her hands still shook, and every few seconds the memory would replay. Doug's falling body, his aborted scream, the sickening thud when his body struck stone. She tilted her face toward the sun, closing her eyes and letting the warmth soak into her skin.

Fresh air filled her lungs, clean and sharp. Wind sighed through trees that clung stubbornly to the rocky slopes, while an eagle circled overhead against peaks that gleamed like cathedral spires. Such simple things—the ability to breathe freely, to feel sunlight on her face, to witness nature's raw beauty. Too often, she took these things for granted.

However, there was no time to linger. She had to return to Sage, but first she needed to rescue Doug's horse, still hobbled outside the cave.

Her mind worked through the logistics. Sage could ride Doug's horse back to Bear's camp. They'd report both deaths and hopefully authorities would arrive soon.

Sucking in a deep breath, Nikki headed toward the front of the cave, following an animal trail that wound between granite boulders and patches of hardy grass. The path led past a corner where overhanging rocks created a sheltered alcove.

Gunner's hackles rose, and he gave a low growl. Fresh bone fragments and fish scales were scattered across the ground where Sage had dumped food waste. Something had been feeding here, something that made her dog uneasy.

Laughing voices grabbed her attention. She looked up to see Sage walking beside a mounted Ryan, both of them relaxed and smiling. They spotted her and called out greetings as Gunner trotted forward to greet Sage.

"We were looking all over for you," Sage said, her face bright with relief. "I made it to the ridge and my cell phone actually worked! I got through to Derek." She gestured toward Ryan. "I ran into him on my way back down. He was out exploring on his own and heard me talking on the phone."

Ryan grinned down at her from Scout's back, his entire demeanor different around the attractive woman. Gone was his awkward fumbling, replaced by an almost shy charm that made him appear years younger. "Lucky I was in the area when she needed help finding you," he added with obvious pride.

"Derek hasn't heard from Jake," Sage continued. "But he wasn't at all worried. Said Jake is one of his best wilderness experts. He told me to stay put and not give up on the operation. He's actually hiking in next week with more supplies."

"Maybe Sage can join us for dinner tonight?" Ryan said, looking at Nikki. "It would be nice for you to have another woman around, and we can use Bear's satellite phone to try calling her boyfriend. Bear won't mind if you ask. He respects you."

They looked so hopeful, so happy. Sage's eyes sparkled and Ryan couldn't seem to stop smiling. Nikki took a steadying breath as she prepared to destroy their good mood.

"Sage," she said, her voice gentle. "I need to tell you something. About Jake. Maybe we should walk away from—"

But Sage's hand shot out, gripping Nikki's arm with surprising strength. "No," she said, her eyes wide with sudden fear. "Tell me now. What happened? Did you find him? Is he hurt?"

The desperate hope in her voice made Nikki's heart clench. There was no gentle way to deliver this news, no private moment that would make it easier. She placed a hand over Sage's.

"I found him," she said softly. "I'm sorry. He's dead."

"That's not right." Sage jerked back. "You're wrong. He's an expert—"

"He fell into a vertical shaft in the cave system. I'm so sorry."

"No, that can't be right. He's too careful. He knows this area." But even as she protested, she dropped to her knees, a low moan escaping as her body began to tremble.

Ryan leaned forward in his saddle, as if trying to comfort her, and Nikki swallowed in dismay. Doug was a murderer who'd gotten exactly what he deserved, but he and Ryan had been close friends, college roommates who'd shared decades of memories, vacations, and hunting trips.

Now she faced the task of delivering news that would shatter Ryan, just as Jake's death had destroyed Sage. She'd already torn Sage's heart out with the truth about Jake. Now she had to inflict the same agony on Ryan.

She stepped closer to Scout, deciding bad news should be delivered quickly. "And Doug also fell to his death, Ryan," she said softly. "I'm sorry to have to tell you that."

"What? But I just saw him an hour ago." Ryan swayed in the saddle as if he might fall off. One hand gripped the horn so tightly his knuckles whitened. "That can't be true," he said.

Both Ryan and Sage were clearly stunned, but Sage's devastation took precedence. While Nikki felt genuine grief for Jake's death, she couldn't muster much sympathy for Doug.

She squeezed Ryan's knee in comfort then hurried back to Sage, where the woman was still down on her knees. "I'm so sorry," she said, removing her jacket to wrap around Sage's shaking shoulders. The mountain air was cold, and shock could accelerate hypothermia.

Gunner's warning bark made her jerk up. Ryan was still sitting on Scout but he was no longer gripping the horn. He was pointing a gun. The bore looked enormous from this angle, a dark deadly muzzle aimed straight at her chest.

She blinked, stunned into silence. This couldn't be happening. Not Ryan, the happy geologist who blushed around Sage and shared his gummies. But there was no mistaking the steel in his hand or the way his finger rested on the trigger. It looked like a .38 revolver, compact enough to hide in a jacket pocket, deadly enough to end her life with a single squeeze.

Fear crawled up her spine as she stared into that unblinking eye of the barrel. Everything about Ryan had changed. His posture, his expression, even the way he held himself in the saddle. The clumsy geologist was gone, replaced by someone who looked perfectly comfortable shooting another human.

"I'm not a good rider," he said, his voice cold. "But I'm a surprisingly good shot."

CHAPTER THIRTY-TWO

Gunner charged toward the mounted man, his body coiling to spring. Every muscle in his frame was focused on one target—Ryan's gun hand, eight feet above. The height disadvantage didn't matter. He'd been trained to take down armed suspects, and his powerful hindquarters bunched for the leap that would carry him to Ryan's wrist and the weapon threatening his partner.

"Call your dog," Ryan snapped, swiveling the gun toward Gunner. "Or he'll be the first one I shoot."

"Quit, Gunner," Nikki hollered, turning sideways and reaching for her Glock, grabbing the distraction Gunner had created. Her hand moved toward her pocket, but she felt nothing. Only the pocketless flannel of her shirt. Dismay washed over her: Her jacket was wrapped around Sage's shoulders ten feet away. Along with her gun.

Gunner skidded to a stop. He backed away stiff-legged, every reluctant step showing his desire to protect. When he reached Nikki's side, he growled with frustration, his eyes never leaving the mounted rider.

Ryan gave a clipped nod. "Good. Now you're both going to turn around and walk back to that crevice."

"What are you doing, Ryan?" The devastation in Sage's voice was replaced by confusion. Then her eyes widened. "Wait, was it you on the buckskin this spring? Were you the one with Elena when she fell? And you rode away?"

Ryan's expression grew even colder, as if the last vestiges of his friendly persona had finally fallen away. What little humanity had remained in his eyes was gone, replaced by something calculating and ruthless. When he spoke, his voice was flat again, like he was discussing the weather.

"Doug understood what was necessary," he said. "Marcus is a wimp who doesn't like violence, always playing the leader, telling me what to do. But Doug was impressed when I pushed Elena off that ridge. He understood that we had to take action instead of sitting around talking about our problems."

His voice dripped with contempt. "She spotted a wolverine on her trail cam. Talked like it was the discovery of the century. Sat by the campfire, nodding and answering my questions as if I gave a damn about her precious research.

"A few drinks and she couldn't wait to tell me her secrets. How the wolverine sighting would bring in federal wildlife investigators. She was glowing with pride, the naive fool. Had no idea she was signing her death warrant. But that wolverine would have stopped our chromium development before it even got started."

Chromium. Nikki gaped at Ryan. That explained everything—the secrecy, the willingness to kill, Doug's government connections. She knew chromium was essential for hardening steel used in military applications, and most of it came from unstable foreign sources. With the current administration pushing for domestic mining of critical defense minerals, a high-grade chromium find could be worth hundreds of millions.

"Once the chromium permits were approved," Ryan said, "this project would have been unstoppable. But if Doug's really dead, it leaves me with no contacts in the mining bureau. My family's legacy, everything we worked for, gone."

He shot a murderous look at Sage, who was still huddled in Nikki's jacket, tears streaming down her face. "But I'll find another way to get those permits. I'm not going to be stopped by bleeding hearts who think animals are more important than prosperity."

His face was a mottled red, spittle forming at the corners of his mouth. "And you," he snarled, glaring at Nikki. "Sticking your nose where it doesn't belong. Bear thinks you're so damn smart, letting you ride off like you own the place. If he'd just kept you close to camp, none of this would have happened!"

Nikki took an involuntary step back. The easygoing man she'd shared meals with had disappeared. Something ruthless and chillingly familiar flickered in his eyes—the same look Doug had worn in the cave. How had she sat around camp beside this killer, laughed at his jokes, never suspecting the darkness beneath his smiling facade?

"Move," Ryan ordered, gesturing with his gun toward the game trail. "We're going back to that crevice where you claim Doug fell. I want to see if he's really dead. And after I confirm what happened, well..." He gave a casual shrug. "Accidents happen."

Nikki's mind scrabbled for options. She and Gunner could rush the horse, but Ryan was mounted with a clear sight line. He'd get off several shots before they reached him. And her legs felt sluggish, as if they belonged to someone else, the adrenaline surge making her movements clumsy.

The thought of returning to that crevice made bile rise in her throat. She could still hear the echo of Doug's scream, could see that yawning dark mouth that had swallowed him whole. Now Ryan wanted to force them back to that same pit, to throw them into the shadows where Doug's broken body lay waiting. The idea of joining his corpse in that black void made her stomach heave.

She pulled Sage to her feet and they stumbled along the game trail. Nikki forced her shoulders to slump, to appear defeated. It was at least a ten-minute walk to the cave. Maybe she could slip her hand around Sage's waist and somehow reach the Glock in her jacket pocket.

She squeezed Sage's arm, trying to grab her attention without alerting Ryan. Sage needed her to understand—a gun was there, within reach, if only Nikki could get to it. But Sage was still too grief-stricken. Her face remained blank, focused inward on her loss.

They took shuffling steps along the rocky trail, pebbles rolling beneath their feet. The air carried the scent of decomposing fish and bones from the spot where Sage and Jake had been dumping their food scraps.

Nikki's senses felt hyper alert. The whiff of food rot, the rasp of Sage's breathing, the click of Scout's shoes echoing like a countdown. Every scent, every sound, registered with crystal clarity. She could feel Ryan's eyes boring into her back, knew his finger rested on the trigger.

He obviously preferred them to walk to the crevice under their own power. But one wrong move would end everything. If he had to kill them now, he could use Scout to drag their bodies to any number of hiding places. Ryan had been exploring these mountains for years and likely knew every sinkhole where bodies could vanish. And where bullet holes wouldn't matter.

Gunner's head suddenly turned to the right, his ears pricked as his nose worked the air, catching a familiar scent. His step slowed, then something brown exploded from the alcove beside them.

Nikki flinched as it streaked past. The animal was low and muscular, the size of a medium dog but built like a bear, with dark brown fur and a distinctive lighter stripe along its sides. Powerful shoulders rippled beneath its coat as it moved with surprising speed.

A wolverine. She'd only seen pictures, but there was no mistaking that compact body and the way it moved. Part weasel, part small bear, all attitude. It cut past Gunner and behind Scout, keen to escape the rocky corner where it had been scavenging.

Scout's ears pinned. The horse that had kicked Gunner was obviously still defensive. He bunched and lashed out with both feet, missing the wolverine but launching his rider high into the air. For a moment, Ryan hung suspended, his arms windmilling as he tried to regain balance. Then he plummeted down, his back smashing against the rock. The impact drove the air from his lungs, silencing his curses and sending his gun clattering.

Gunner charged forward, his attention torn between the fleeing wolverine and the man on the ground.

"Watch him," Nikki said, pointing to Ryan. She scooped up the gun while Gunner stopped beside Ryan, teeth bared.

Nikki checked on Scout, worried he'd bolt, but he stood stock still, eyeing Ryan as if puzzled why his rider was on the ground. And despite Nikki's pounding heart, a smile tugged at the corners of her mouth. Thirty seconds ago they'd been helpless victims marching toward a horrible grave. Now their would-be executioner lay flat on his back, defeated by a timely kick.

Bear truly had some good horses.

CHAPTER THIRTY-THREE

The helicopter's rotor wash flattened the meadow grass as the Forest Service aircraft settled onto the natural landing zone. White fuselage gleamed against green striping and the USFS badge that marked it as federal authority. The turbine whine decreased as engines spooled down, replaced by the metallic ticking and pinging of cooling aircraft.

The morning sun had already burned off the dew, and warm light bathed the camp. The horses fidgeted on the picket line, eyeing the alien helicopter with a mixture of alarm and curiosity. Even now, as relative quiet returned, the contrast between wilderness and government machinery felt jarring.

Two federal agents emerged from the aircraft, their boots hitting the ground with a purposeful thud. They moved with the confidence of professionals accustomed to handling dangerous situations in remote locations. Within moments, they had taken custody of the two prisoners from Bear, checking restraints and conducting a brief security assessment.

Then each agent escorted a prisoner across the uneven ground toward the waiting helicopter. They maintained proper spacing, hands positioned near their weapons despite the suspects being cuffed. Ryan walked beside his escort with his head high, defiance radiating from every step, while Marcus shuffled along, showing the defeated posture of a man whose world had collapsed overnight.

Ryan shot venomous looks at Nikki, Bear, and Sage as he passed.

"You people destroyed everything my family worked for," he snarled, twisting against the agent's grip. "Generations of sacrifice! And you threw it away, for what? Some stupid animal!"

The agent urged him forward when he tried to continue, but his bitter accusations still carried. Behind him, Marcus walked with shoulders slumped, staring at his feet and avoiding eye contact. His repeated protests had become tiresome: "I never knew Elena was murdered. I thought it was an accident."

Nikki studied him, her investigative instincts still active despite her exhaustion. His body language suggested genuine shock, but Justin always stressed that some criminals were exceptional actors. The timing of Marcus's horror seemed quite convenient.

A third figure approached them, a woman in a pressed khaki uniform with federal badge and nameplate reading Special Agent Rodriguez. She wore a tactical vest with radio and duty gear. Her wide-brimmed ranger hat and aviator sunglasses gave her an authoritative bearing, though her expression carried concern rather than bureaucratic coldness.

"Mr. Hutchins," she said, addressing Bear with a firm handshake. "Agent Rodriguez, Forest Service Law Enforcement. Hell of a situation you handled here."

Bear shifted uncomfortably under the praise. "Nikki's the one who figured it all out. I just provided the satellite phone."

Rodriguez turned to Nikki, her gaze curious. "Ms. Drake? Your report over the phone was impressive. Walk me through how you brought the suspect back to camp."

Nikki explained their return journey from the mining area. Sage had ridden Doug's horse—a steady, reliable mount that seemed to sense the young woman's grief and responded with extra gentleness. Ryan had been forced back onto Scout with his hands bound by a lead rope, his constant complaints ignored. Scout seemed to take great pleasure in walking too close to trees and bumping his rider's legs.

"I brought up the rear," Nikki continued, "keeping Ryan in sight the whole time." And this time she'd made certain to keep her Glock within reach.

"What about the other suspect?"

Bear stepped forward. "Marcus was already at camp with me when they arrived. His reaction to the news about Ryan and Elena's murder was..." He paused, choosing his words carefully. "Seemed genuine. But we weren't taking chances."

"The phone call went out immediately," Nikki added. "As soon as we had Ryan and Marcus secured, Bear contacted your dispatch. We knew we needed professional backup fast."

Rodriguez made notes on a small pad. "And overnight security?"

"Bear and I took turns on watch," Nikki said, feeling the exhaustion in her bones. "Three-hour shifts. Both suspects were restrained with climbing rope, and kept apart."

"Excellent," Rodriguez said, turning to Sage. "Ms. Crux, I can have you on that helicopter in five minutes. Get you to medical care and away from all this."

Sage's pale complexion betrayed her grief, but her expression remained resolute. "Thank you, but I can't be in that confined space with *him*." She gestured toward Ryan without looking directly at the helicopter. "I'd rather ride down with Bear and Nikki. And they'll probably need help now that there are five riderless horses."

She turned to Bear with questioning eyes. "If that's all right with you?"

"Of course it's all right," Bear said, his solemn face softening. "More than all right. I'd be grateful for the help."

Nikki found herself surprised, and impressed. Just five days ago, Sage had been helping Jake set trip wires for Bear's horses. Now she was offering to help those same animals. And most people would have jumped at the chance to escape this mountain and its tragic memories. Sage's thoughtfulness in the midst of her devastation showed loyalty and resilience.

Agent Rodriguez looked at Bear. "Outstanding work managing a dangerous situation. Your experience shows."

Bear shook his head, gesturing toward Nikki. "Like I said, she's the one who figured it all out. I just kept the camp running." He glanced down at Gunner, who sat beside them. "And her partner here has a hell of a nose for tracking. I'll admit, at first I wasn't keen on having him around. But that dog has good manners, and he proved himself real useful."

Rodriguez nodded and put away her notebook. "Well, I'll be contacting you all again for formal reports. As for the bodies, we'll need to coordinate recovery operations with the county search and rescue team. The location you described—that vertical shaft in the cave system—is going to require technical rope specialists and cave experts."

The agent looked toward the mountain where the mining area lay hidden. "Weather permitting, we're looking at a minimum three-day operation. Maybe longer depending on what our advance team finds when they assess the site. The good news is Jake's body should be recoverable, based on what was described."

Rodriguez's expression grew more serious. "Doug Lohnes's remains in that crevice will be significantly more challenging. I'll be honest. Full recovery might not be possible given the risk."

Nikki crossed her arms, feeling a shiver run down her spine. She glanced at Sage and found the young woman staring back, her eyes haunted. They both understood how close they'd come to being the bodies that would never be recovered from that deep tomb.

The helicopter's engines spooled up again, rotor blades starting their rotation. Pine scent mixed with aviation fuel as the sun climbed higher. An eagle circled above with magnificent indifference to the human drama playing out below.

"Time to go," a man's voice called over the increasing noise of the helicopter engines.

Rodriguez strode back across the meadow, ducking as she approached the aircraft. She paused at the door and touched the brim of her hat in acknowledgment.

As the aircraft lifted off with its cargo of killers and questions, Nikki patted Gunner's head. His fur was warm and reassuring, and she felt her body relax. The knot of anxiety that had lived in her chest for days finally began to unwind. Ryan and Marcus were no longer her concern. And she certainly had answers for the insurance company.

The helicopter disappeared beyond the ridge, its mechanical noise gradually swallowed by the vast mountain silence. What remained was the familiar chatter of a squirrel scolding them from a nearby pine, mingled with the gentle babbling of the stream.

And the impatient pawing of horses ready to head home.

CHAPTER THIRTY-FOUR

Evening light filtered through the tree branches in Nikki and Justin's backyard, casting shadows across the lawn. Warm air carried the mingled scents of jasmine from the flower beds and smoke from the grill where Justin tended two thick steaks. Their privacy fence created a city sanctuary, a stark contrast to the mountain wilderness Nikki had left a month ago.

She set down a platter of vegetables on the patio table. Gunner immediately looked up from his spot near the fence where the neighbor's tabby cat had wandered, ever hopeful that supper would be shared.

"Almost ready," Justin called, flipping the steaks amid a flare of juice.

Nikki settled into her usual chair and grabbed the chance to check her messages. She and Gunner had been busy all day tracking down a potbellied pig that had dug under its owner's gate and was terrorizing a suburban neighborhood. The pig had finally been cornered behind a strip mall, squealing indignantly when Gunner herded it into a crate.

She scrolled through emails and notifications, most of them routine follow-ups and the usual requests for background checks. She paused at a message from a name she recognized: Professor Miguel Vasquez, Elena's husband.

Dear Ms. Drake,

I can't thank you enough for your bravery in solving the mystery of Elena's death. The more I learn about what happened, the more I realize how dangerous it was. Elena would have been so grateful to know someone cared enough to find the truth.

I thought you might be interested in the attached video from Elena's recovered trail camera, along with some links to stories about the aftermath of your investigation.

With my deepest gratitude, Professor Miguel Vasquez

Nikki clicked on the attachment. The image was surprisingly clear. A wolverine sniffing at a low bush, its distinctive face barely a foot away. She could make out the golden highlight of its dark brown fur, the powerful jaw, its intelligent eyes.

But it was the background that made her stomach lurch. Those granite boulders were disturbingly familiar. This was outside the cave where she and Gunner had fled, close to the crevice where Doug was still lying.

"Tough news?" Justin asked, leaving the grill and moving to her side.

"Just some follow-up from the Marble Mountain case." She positioned the phone so he could see the video. "Elena's husband sent this from the trail cam we found."

Justin watched as the wolverine sniffed around the bush, its powerful frame moving with surprising grace. "Incredible," he said. "It's one of the most elusive animals in North America. They can travel fifty miles in a single day and have jaws strong enough to chew through frozen bone. Most people go their entire lives without seeing one in the wild. And now you have your own video."

He smiled, and she caught that combination of sharp intelligence and rugged good looks that never failed to make her pulse quicken. Those dark eyes that missed nothing, the way he could make her feel better even after the worst days and his genuine love for animals—it was a potent combination that reminded her why she'd fallen for him in the first place.

Her gaze held his. "And Sonja was right after all. She sensed an animal around Elena but thought it was a dog. No wonder it was worth killing for. Not the animal itself, but what its presence meant for any development plans."

She pressed on the first of the two links Elena's husband had included. A news article loaded, the headline reading: "Rare Wolverine Sighting Sparks Conservation Excitement."

The recent discovery of a wolverine in California's Marble Mountains has caused considerable excitement among conservationists, animal rights groups, and researchers. Derek Stone's environmental coalition is calling the sighting "proof that these pristine areas deserve permanent protection." The University of California is posthumously honoring Dr. Elena Vasquez, the researcher whose trail camera captured the rare footage before her tragic death.

While rumors persist about a chromium discovery in the area, federal officials continue to deny any mining interests in the region. Ryan Torres has been charged with Dr. Elena Vasquez's murder, with Marcus Webb facing charges as an accomplice.

Justin read over her shoulder, and she could feel him stiffen as he was reminded of the dangers she'd faced. He placed a hand on her arm, his grip tightening as he processed the details about Ryan's charges and the conspiracy. The pressure was almost painful before he caught himself and gentled his touch, his fingers becoming a reassuring caress instead of a protective grip.

She clicked on the second link. A blog post by Sage Crux, who already had thousands of followers.

"The Marble Mountains should remain a pristine sanctuary for generations to come," Sage had written in her latest post. *"It's a place where wildlife and humans can coexist respectfully. For those who want to experience this incredible wilderness, I highly recommend Bear Hutchins. This renowned trail guide offers spring trips on amazing horses and teaches visitors how to enjoy these sacred spaces while leaving no trace. Thanks to people like Bear, we can preserve these mountains while still sharing their beauty."*

It was impressive how Sage had channeled her grief into something positive. The young woman had found a way to honor Jake's memory while pursuing her original career goal of environmental education. Instead of the confrontational activism that had drawn her to Derek Stone's coalition, she was building bridges between conservationists and outdoor enthusiasts. Her blog promoted responsible wilderness access while advocating for protection, the kind of balanced approach that could create lasting change.

Nikki tucked her phone away, wanting to focus on the evening with Justin rather than dwelling on the past. The insurance case was closed, justice was being served, and life was moving forward.

Justin returned to the grill, and she watched him with appreciation. The concern he'd shown when he noticed her reaction to the video, his natural confidence whether facing dangerous criminals or simply cooking dinner. He was a hard-nosed detective who dealt with LA's worst, yet he could be infinitely gentle.

They were both dedicated to helping people, he through the justice system and she through private investigation, and their demanding careers left little time for leisure. But that made evenings like this even more precious.

She only had one question for her thoughtful lover.

"You know," she said, leaning back in her chair, "Bear called me last week to thank me for the insurance report. Says his premiums were slashed. He's ecstatic. He also asked if I was the one who sent a truckload of carrots to Brownie and Scout, with more than enough for all his horses."

"A truckload?" Justin's expression was perfectly neutral, that stone-cold cop look he'd perfected after years of interrogating suspects. His face revealed nothing. The same impassive mask he wore when questioning hardened criminals trying to lie their way out of murder charges.

But Nikki knew him too well. She caught the twitch at the corner of his mouth, barely perceptible, but that tiny tell was as good as a confession.

"I told Bear I had no idea where the carrots came from," she said. "But I think maybe I do."

Justin just smiled.

OTHER BOOKS BY BEV PETTERSEN:

Grave Instinct (Nikki Drake K9 Mystery)
Repent (Nikki Drake K9 Mystery)
Bone Trail (Nikki Drake K9 Mystery)
Dead Man's Trail (Nikki Drake K9 Mystery)
False Start (Nikki Drake K9 Mystery)
Jockeys and Jewels
Color My Horse
Fillies and Females
Thoroughbreds and Trailer Trash
Studs and Stilettos
Riding For Redemption
A Scandalous Husband
Backstretch Baby
Shadows of the Mountain
Along Came A Cowboy
A Pony For Christmas (Novella)

About The Author

USA *Today Bestselling Author* Bev Pettersen is a three-time nominee in the National Readers Choice Award as well as the winner of many other international awards including the Reader Views Reviewer's Choice Award, Aspen Gold Reader's Choice Award, Write Touch Readers' Award, Kirkus Recommended Read, and a HOLT Medallion Award of Merit. She competed on the Alberta Thoroughbred race circuit and is an Equestrian Canada certified coach.

Bev lives in Nova Scotia with her family, humans and four-legged, and when she's not writing novels, she's riding. If you'd like to know about special offers or just want to say hi, please visit her at http://www.BevPettersen.com